Almost a Bride

Almost a Bride

A Montana Born Brides Novella

Sarah Mayberry

TULE
PUBLISHING

Almost a Bride
© Copyright 2014 Sarah Mayberry
Tule Publishing First Printing, May 2018

The Tule Publishing Group, LLC

ALL RIGHTS RESERVED

No part of this book may be used or reproduced in any manner whatsoever without written permission except in the case of brief quotations embodied in critical articles and reviews.

This is a work of fiction. Names, characters, places, and incidents are products of the author's imagination or are used fictitiously. Any resemblance to actual events, locales, organizations or persons, living or dead, is entirely coincidental.

ISBN 978-1-949068-23-8

Dedication

A huge thanks to the lovely Lilian Darcy and Jane Porter for thinking of me for Tule, and to the rest of the talented ladies who are contributing to the Brides series. Special, super-duper thanks to Trish Morey, for making me laugh and hanging with me in the writing trench. And, as always, I couldn't do what I do without Chris and Max by my side. You boys are my salvation.

Dear Reader,

There was so many things I enjoyed about writing this book. I loved writing for Tule Publishing's Montana Born imprint, loved all the amazing women who were working alongside me in this Spring Brides series, loved having Jane Porter cheering me on from the sidelines, and particularly loved having the hilarious and so clever Trish Morey as my wingwoman as we worked together to create a family and history for our twins, Tara and Scarlett Buck.

I can't remember who suggested our heroines be twins, but once the idea took root Trish and I were off and running. The emails flew back and forth as we discussed who our twins were and how they saw the world and how they were different from each other. It was Trish's idea that her heroine be named after Scarlett from *Gone with The Wind*, so of course my heroine had to have a *Wind* reference, too.

I'm not sure if it was the fact that Tara is named after a house, not a person, that gave me the idea that she was the sensible sister. Capable and practical and dependable. Deep down inside, though, Tara is just as scared, impulsive and spontaneous as the next woman – especially if the next woman is her twin. I loved helping Tara understand herself, and I especially loved helping her and her man, Reid, work out what was good and right and amazing for both of them.

If you haven't had a chance to read it yet, don't forget to grab Scarlett's story, *Second Chance Bride*! That Trish Morey is a funny lady, and I'm sure it will leave you smiling. In the meantime, I hope you enjoy Tara and Reid's story.

Happy reading,

Sarah Mayberry

Chapter One

REID DALTON PUMPED gas into his GMC pickup, one ear tuned to the conversation going on between his friends inside the truck. Grant was giving Brett a hard time for missing an easy layup during the basketball game they'd just finished, and Brett was serving it straight back at him with both barrels.

Reid grinned to himself, feeling pleasantly tired after an hour of charging up and down the court, trouncing the Bozeman Fire Department team. The informal competition between the police department and the firefighters had become a regular thing over the past few months. Reid wasn't sure which part of their weekly matchups he enjoyed the most—the rapid-fire pace of the game itself, or the inevitable shit giving and taking that occurred afterward.

"You want to know my opinion?" he asked as the pump clicked off, signaling the tank was full.

"Not particularly," Brett said, which earned him a guffaw from Grant.

"You both need to lift your games. Drink less beer, run a

few more miles," Reid said.

Grant made a rude noise, while Brett gave him a one-fingered salute. Reid was still laughing as he headed into the gas station to pay the cashier.

Then he saw the couple exiting the motel next door to the Gas-And-Go Mart and his step faltered.

The girl he didn't recognize, but she was young and blonde and clinging to her man as though her very life depended on it. Reid watched as Simon Garfield said something before kissing her in a way that left no doubt whatsoever as to the nature of their relationship.

Damn.

Just… damn.

Tara would be devastated.

For a moment he was frozen as he absorbed all the implications of what he'd just witnessed. Tara had been planning the wedding for the past few months and as her patrol partner, there was precious little Reid wasn't privy to. Like the fact that Tara and Simon planned on having the reception at Le Petit Chateau in Bozeman, and that Tara was limiting her attendants to just her twin, Scarlett, and that today she had an appointment at Marietta's one and only bridal salon to pick out her wedding dress…

Belatedly he glanced back at the car, hoping the other guys hadn't seen, but they were both frowning, staring out the windshield at the sordid little drama unfolding in the parking lot next door. There wasn't a doubt in Reid's mind that they recognized Tara's fiancé. They'd all attended the engagement party Tara and Simon held back in February.

Reid mouthed a four-letter word.

What a nightmare.

Simon and the blonde were climbing into separate cars. Reid automatically noted the blonde's license plate before she turned onto the highway, heading toward Marietta.

She was a local, then.

Simon waited until a few cars blew past before following suit.

Reid shook his head in disgust before heading inside to pay for the gas. Both the guys were silent when he returned to the truck. Brett waited until they were heading for Marietta themselves before speaking up.

"What are you going to tell her?"

Reid didn't take his eyes off the road. "The truth."

Because no way was he sitting on this. The last thing he would ever want to do is hurt Tara—the thought literally made his gut ache—but there was no way he was going to look the other way and tell himself it was none of his business.

She'd want to know. Even if the truth was going to tear her world apart.

"When is the wedding?" Grant asked.

"Four months," Reid said.

There was a profound silence in the car as they all processed that particular piece of information.

"You think she has any idea…?" Brett asked.

Reid shot him a hard look. Tara was the most straight-up, no-bull person he knew. She wouldn't live with that kind of deceit. Wouldn't tolerate it for a second.

"Yeah. You're right," Brett said. "Stupid question. Forget I said anything."

Silence reigned for the remainder of the twenty-minute drive into town. Reid dropped both guys off at Brett's place, where Grant had left his car.

"Listen… give me a chance to talk to Tara, okay?" he said after the guys had hauled their gear out of the back of the truck.

Grant looked offended. "Like we're going to be running around telling anyone what we saw. Give us a little credit."

Brett simply nodded. They all knew that Grant told his wife, Sally, everything sooner or later, something that was only underlined by the dull red flush coloring the other man's face. Once Sally knew, it would simply be a matter of time before the story spread like wildfire.

"See you guys tomorrow," Reid said before pulling away from the curb.

His jaw set, he drove straight into the heart of town. The pink and white facade of Married in Marietta came up on his left and he pulled into the nearest empty parking spot. Then he sat and stared out the windshield and tried to work out how he was going to do this. What he was going to say.

Because he needed to do and say something pretty

quick—he figured he had a couple of hours max before Grant blabbed to his wife and the phone lines of Marietta began burning up with the news that Simon Garfield was cheating on Tara Buck. Tara needed to know so she could brace herself for the oncoming storm.

First things first, though. Pulling out his phone, he called the station and had a quick chat with Dave on the desk. Sixty seconds later, he had the registration details for the car the blonde had been driving. Paige Donovan. One mystery solved.

It was Saturday afternoon, and there were plenty of people out and about, but Reid didn't register any of them as he stared into the distance. He was too busy remembering the look on Tara's face when she'd told him Simon had asked her to marry him. Her smile had been shy as she'd shown Reid the modest solitaire diamond her fiancé had bought to seal the deal. Reid had said all the right things, asked all the right questions, but there had been a hot feeling in his chest and it had taken him a few minutes to own it for what it was—jealousy. A fruitless and useless emotion, given who Tara was and what they were to each other: partners and friends, nothing more, nothing less. He had no right to be jealous of the man in her life.

And yet he had been, and sitting here now, he couldn't deny that even though he dreaded the upcoming conversation, there was a part of him that was relieved because he wouldn't have to stand in a church in four months' time and watch Tara marry someone else.

Which pretty much made him a selfish bastard of the highest order, he figured.

He shoved the car door open, walking away from his own thoughts.

His heart started to pound as he approached the salon. He wiped his hands down the sides of his shorts. Man, this was going to be hard. How on earth was he going to deliver such a painful blow to someone who deserved only happiness?

Gritting his teeth, he pushed open the door to the salon, entering a plush-carpeted world painted in soft neutrals. Fragile-looking velvet upholstered chairs dotted the space, along with tall vases filled with flowers. The walls were lined with racks bursting with white frothy dresses, a veritable sea of satin and tulle and silk, and a crystal chandelier fractured the light from half a dozen globes overhead.

A couple of women were browsing the racks, and they turned to stare at him in much the same way he imagined they might if he'd wandered into the women's restroom. A slim, middle-aged woman dressed entirely in black bustled out from behind the counter, an alarmed expression on her face.

"Hello. Can I help you?" she asked.

"I'm looking for Tara Buck. She was supposed to be here today, trying on dresses," Reid said.

He was suddenly very aware of his mussed hair, sweat-dampened T-shirt and shorts. Probably he should have taken the time to change into something more appropriate before coming here.

"And you are...?"

It occurred to him belatedly that she was worried he was the groom.

"I'm a friend. We work together."

"I'll just check and see what I can do for you," she said, giving him a dubious head to toe.

"Reid."

He turned toward the familiar voice—and forgot to breathe.

Tara wore a flowing white gown that hugged her body in all the right places—breasts, waist, hips. The way the lustrous fabric wrapped around her mid-section emphasized how slender she was, while a neckline with a little dip in the middle drew his attention to her breasts and the bare expanse of her shoulders. A froth of lace was pinned to her upswept blond hair, completing the bridal ensemble.

She was beautiful, absolutely heart-stoppingly gorgeous, and for a moment he could do nothing but stare.

"What on earth are you doing here?" Tara asked, laughing uncertainly. "I'm pretty sure you're not supposed to see the bride before the wedding. Isn't it supposed to be bad luck or something?"

Scarlett, Tara's non-identical twin, joined them, dressed more conventionally in jeans and a T-shirt, her crazy red hair pulled back in a ponytail.

"That's the groom, doofus," she said. "You are the worst bride ever. How can you be getting married and know so little about weddings? Lucky Mitch made an honest woman of me in April or you wouldn't have a seasoned pro around to show you the ropes." Her gaze was curious as she glanced at Reid. "Hey, Dalton. What are you doing here?"

"I need to speak to Tara."

Tara's smile faded. "Why do you have that look in your eye?"

"What look?" Scarlett asked, frowning.

"His cop look. Has something happened? Oh, God, don't tell me something's happened to Simon?" Tara's eyes were wide now, and she pressed a hand to her stomach as though bracing herself for bad news.

Reid glanced around, aware that everyone in the salon had stopped to stare at them.

"Simon is fine." For now, anyway. Reid wasn't prepared to guarantee his future good health, however. "Is there somewhere private we can talk?"

"What's going on?" Tara asked, taking a step toward him.

No way was he doing this out here, with all these people watching. He turned to the sales assistant.

"Do you have an office?"

"Yes. It's out the back…"

Reid was already moving, reaching for Tara's elbow as he

hustled her toward the rear of the store.

"You're freaking me out, Reid," Tara said.

She came with him willingly enough, though, because she trusted him. Trusted the hours they'd spent in the patrol car together and the confidences they'd shared and the deep knowledge they had of one another.

And he was about to break her heart.

"I'll just wait out here, then," Scarlett called after them, clearly miffed to be excluded from whatever was going on.

Reid spotted an open door, ducking his head in to find a desk, along with a filing cabinet and bookcase. He pulled Tara in after him and kicked the door shut.

They stood there eyeing each other for a long beat. Then he took a deep breath and did what needed to be done.

"I just saw Simon leaving the motel out on 98 with another woman."

FOR A HEARTBEAT Tara didn't understand what Reid was saying. She was so disconcerted by his sudden appearance during her dress appointment, her brain seemed to be on vacation. He looked so out of place in the salon, with his mussed-up dark hair, broad-shoulders and lean, hard body dressed in work-out gear.

Then she blinked and his words hit home. She opened her mouth to deny him, to insist that he must have gotten it wrong, but Reid was watching her with his coffee-dark eyes and she knew that he wouldn't be here telling her this if it wasn't true. If he wasn't sure.

"Tell me," she said.

"We were heading home from our weekly game—"

"We?"

"Brett and Grant."

She closed her eyes for a long beat. Grant's wife was the biggest motormouth she knew, hands down.

"Did he see them as well?"

She didn't need to refer to Grant by name; she and Reid had been talking in short-hand since their first week on patrol together.

"They both did."

"Okay." She nodded, gesturing for him to resume filling in the blanks. She needed the facts—all of them—before she tried to work out how to respond, how to feel, what to do.

"Maybe you should sit down," Reid said, shoving the wheeled chair her way.

"I'm fine. Tell me the rest."

"There's not much more. We stopped at the Gas-and-Go Mart out on 98, and they came out of the motel next door and drove off in separate cars."

"They were definitely together?" It was a feeble straw, but she owed it to herself—to the future she'd had planned—to grasp it.

"Yes."

Reid's terse reply and the way he broke eye contact with

her said more than any words could. She wondered what he'd seen. Them kissing? Some kind of clinch?

"Who is she?" she asked.

Because she knew without asking that he would have gotten the other woman's plates. She would have done the same for him if she had been in his shoes.

"Paige Donovan. Do you know her?"

Paige Donovan.

She needed the chair then, one hand already reaching for it as her knees suddenly didn't work anymore. She leaned forward in the chair, dizzy with the implications of what he'd just revealed.

Reid crouched down in front of her, trying to see her face. "You're not going to faint, are you?"

No. But there was a good chance she might throw up.

"She's one of his students," she said, somehow getting the words past the tightness in her throat.

She'd heard the girl's name often enough to know. Paige had been a thorn in Simon's side since she'd walked into his class at the beginning of the year. Up until recently, he'd complained about her on a weekly basis.

Reid's expression was stony. "How old is she?"

Something was tickling her face and she realized she was still wearing the stupid veil. Reaching up, she dragged it free, not caring that the pins pulled her hair with them.

"I don't know. She's a senior. Seventeen. Maybe eighteen."

Simon was twenty-eight, two years older than Tara. The age of consent in Montana was sixteen, so even if Paige was only seventeen, he was probably in the clear legally.

Morally… he was toast. On so many levels. He was the girl's teacher—and he was Tara's fiancé. The man she had lived with for two years. The man she'd planned to start a family with, grow old alongside…

Reid took both her hands in his. Hers were icy, his warm and strong.

"Whatever you need, I'm here, okay?"

There was a gravelly note to his voice that made her throat get even tighter. His eyes were full of sympathy, and a worried frown creased his forehead.

"Thanks."

Her gaze dropped to his strong thighs, exposed thanks to his workout shorts. He had a tan, she couldn't help noticing. When on earth did he have time to get a tan, in between pulling shifts at Bozeman PD with her and helping out his parents in their apple orchard?

The absurdity of the thought—the stupid, inappropriate randomness of it—almost made her laugh. She was noticing Reid Dalton's thighs now, of all times?

It's easier than dealing with the truth.

Indeed.

It was tempting to cling to his hands, to use them as an anchor, but this was her mess. Her life. Her fiancé.

She eased back in the seat, slipping her hands free from

his, suddenly overwhelmingly aware of the weight of the dress she was wearing. Not so many minutes ago, the heavy satin fabric and the dress's boning had felt comforting, supportive, substantial. Now it felt like a cage. A trap.

She stood. "I need to get out of this dress."

He stood, too, but she was already pushing past him, opening the door. Her sister was hovering near the change rooms, arms crossed over her chest, her expression worried.

"What's going on?" she asked as Tara marched toward her.

"Help me out of this thing. I want it off," Tara said.

She offered her sister her back, every muscle tense as she waited for the hiss of the zipper.

"Can you please tell me what's going on?" Scarlett asked, her voice scared now.

It hit Tara that her sister was probably imagining the worst—death or injury for someone they loved. Nothing as small and seedy as the truth.

"Simon has been having an affair with one of his students," Tara said.

There was a profound silence behind her. Then she felt the tug of the zipper being undone. Wordlessly she walked into the change room, Scarlett hard on her heels. Her sister didn't say anything, simply shut the door. For the first time Tara was grateful that their mother hadn't been able to attend today's appointment, the symptoms from her recently diagnosed Parkinson's disease having taxed her severely over the last few days. Tammy Buck had never been good in a crisis, and she would be cursing up a storm and weeping and hollering right now if she were here, sucking up all the oxygen in the room and leaving nothing for anyone else.

Instead, there was only Scarlett working silently to help her out of the dress. Only when the satin was piled on the chair in the corner did her sister open her arms, her eyes filled with sadness. Tara's shoulders sagged, and she fell into her twin's embrace.

"I'm so sorry," Scarlett said, her voice raw.

Out of all the people in the world, only Scarlett knew how truly awful this moment was.

Tara had worked all her life to avoid her mother's fate. She had been careful. She had been prudent. She had been wise.

And yet here she was.

Disengaging from her sister's embrace, she reached for her clothes.

"Let's get out of here."

Chapter Two

Somehow Tara managed to hold in her tears until she was safely home, the door shut between her and the world. Scarlett had been adamant about coming home with her, and Reid had hovered while she'd made her excuses to Lisa Renee, the manager of Married in Marietta, but Tara had convinced them both that there was no merit to be had in hashing over everything.

Not that Reid would want to hash over anything. He wasn't the type to talk for talking's sake. He would have sat vigil with her if she'd asked, though. But she wanted to be alone when Simon came home. It was humiliating enough that the whole town would soon know of her fiancé's betrayal; she didn't need witnesses to the ugly little scene that was sure to ensue.

Scarlett had been harder to shake, but Tara's insistence that this was something she needed to do alone had finally sunk in. Her twin couldn't lessen this pain or take it away. This was all Tara's.

Tara glanced around the living room of the town house

she and Simon shared, taking in the classic rolled-arm cream-colored couch with its oversized cushions, the recycled Oregon coffee table they'd picked up at a craft fair, the antique oil lamp that had once been her grandmother's.

It all looked so nice and neat and perfect. Like a page out of a Pottery Barn catalogue.

She drew in a shuddering breath. Simon was supposedly playing golf with a buddy this afternoon. He'd told her he probably wouldn't be home until after three when he kissed her goodbye. Angry tears filled her eyes as she imagined him putting his golf bag in the back of his car—along with whatever it was a person took to a motel room when he planned on cheating on his bride-to-be. Condoms, maybe. Perhaps a bottle of wine, or a small gift for his girlfriend.

Girl being the operative word.

Tears rolled down her face as the reaction she'd fought so hard to hold off washed over her. Her body shook, her teeth chattering with the force of her anger and hurt. How could Simon do this to her? How could he lie in bed next to her, night after night, talking and laughing and, yes, making love with her, while all the while he was bedding one of his students?

It was beyond her. The man she'd lived with for two years simply wasn't capable of this kind of betrayal. He was decent. He was gentle. He was thoughtful and a little stubborn and sometimes overly cautious.

He was also a fantasy, apparently. A figment of her imagination. Because her Simon—the one she'd thought she was going to marry, the man she'd thought she'd spend the rest of her life with—didn't exist. She'd been sharing her life with some other person. A man she didn't know at all. A man who was capable of undressing one of his students—a girl who not so long ago had been wearing a training bra and taking driving lessons and giggling over posters of One Direction and Zac Efron—and lying down with her in a cheap motel in the middle of nowhere.

Bile burned the back of her throat. She wiped away the tears with the backs of her hands, then marched into the bedroom. Bundling the duvet in her arms, she dragged it off the bed and kicked it into the corner. The sheets came next. The pillow cases resisted her efforts to strip them from the pillows and she sobbed with fury as she wrenched first one, then the other free. The duvet cover was liberated, then she took the lot into the laundry room and stuffed it all into the washing machine with vicious, angry jabs. She poured in too much detergent, then slapped the machine on.

Then she slid down the wall until her ass hit the floor. Head bowed, she cried until there were no more tears, and all that was left was a hollow ache in her chest.

Had her mother felt like this the day she came home to find Tara's father gone, leaving her to raise two thirteen-year-old girls alone? Had she felt sick and sad and angry all at the same time? As though the rug had been pulled out from beneath her?

Tara didn't know. She'd never had a conversation with her mother on the subject. In fact, she'd assiduously avoided it, a tough ask given her mother's inability to let go and move on, even after thirteen years.

Tara and Scarlett had grown into womanhood steeped in stories of their father's reckless charm and sense of adventure, every tale ending with the same bitter, wounded observation from their mother—that man had no business getting married.

Despite the fact that she'd had no contact with her father once the divorce was final—her father's choice—Tara had been old enough when he left to have her own memories to draw on. She could remember piggyback rides and impulsive day trips to far-flung parts of the state and being showered with presents for no reason whatsoever, simply because their father felt like it. She could remember his magnetic warmth and infectious laughter, the way people used to gravitate to him. And she could remember his restlessness and dark silences, the way he used to look at her and Scarlett sometimes, as though the walls were pressing in on him.

Most of all she remembered the pain of discovering that he'd lied to her, that his promises had been worth nothing, and that he'd chosen a short redhead with big breasts over her and her sister and their mother.

And yet here she was, staring the same betrayal in the face, despite the fact that she'd done her level best to learn from her mother's mistakes and pick a man she could trust.

An earnest man. A man who laughed quietly, who loved history, who had a genuine passion for teaching. A man who was steady and goodhearted.

Safe.

She'd had three serious boyfriends since she started dating in her late teens and a couple of not-so-serious ones, but Simon had been the best of them. Or so she'd believed.

Her tears dried. The hypnotic chug-chug of the washing machine lulled her into a dull-eyed trance as she waited for Simon to return home. She breathed, she tried not to think. She waited.

She had no idea how much time passed before she heard his car in the driveway. Slowly she pushed herself to her feet. The sound of the front door opening and closing echoed through the townhouse.

"Hey, I'm back. How was your shopping trip?" Simon called. "Did you find your princess-for-a-day dress?"

She studied the floor for a second. Then she lifted her chin. He was tossing his car keys onto the hall table when she entered the living room, an easy smile on his face. His chinos were crisp, his dark blond hair perfectly in place.

"Hey—" His smile dropped like a rock when he saw her face. He took a step toward her, one hand extended. "What's wrong, baby?"

She saw the exact moment that it hit him that she knew. His step faltered. His hand wavered in the air before falling to his side.

"You have half an hour to pack whatever you need, then I'm having the locks changed." Her voice sounded distant and foreign even to her own ears.

The color drained from his face. "I can explain."

"You don't need to. Reid saw you and Paige Donovan leaving a motel. That pretty much covers it, don't you think?" Tara took out her phone and opened the timer function, spinning the dial until she had thirty minutes showing. She tapped the screen to start it off.

"Thirty minutes," she said, heading for the front door.

He grabbed her arm as she walked past, his grip urgent.

"Please, Tara. You have to understand. I tried so hard. I didn't want any of this to happen. You have to believe me."

"Take your hands off me."

"It was a mistake. It only happened this one time, I swear. And it will never happen again—"

He knew her history, knew about her father. And still he'd done this to her.

"Take. Your. Hands. Off. Me."

His grip loosened and she pulled free. Eyes straight ahead, she strode to the door.

She could hear him breathing as she pulled it open, panting as though he'd just run a race. Panicking over the fact that his whole world was about to implode around him, no doubt.

She shut the door firmly behind herself, then walked to the nearest flower bed and threw up.

REID DROVE STRAIGHT out to his parents' place after leaving Tara. She didn't want his help, but it didn't feel right to simply walk away. Yet that was what he was doing, because he didn't have any other options.

He passed the dusty sign for Dalton Orchards and turned into the gravel driveway. Apple trees marched either side of the winding road, escorting him all the way to the simple white-washed farmhouse and outbuildings that had been home to Daltons for three generations.

He parked his car beneath the old oak tree and went into the main house. He could hear his mother in the kitchen, banging pots around, a sure sign she was pissed about something. She barely glanced at him as he entered, returning to whatever she was doing in the cupboard next to the oven. He headed straight to the fridge for the pitcher of iced tea his mother always kept there.

"What's he done now?" he asked.

"I caught him up a ladder, checking on the apple scab on those trees down near the western fence." Judy Dalton's voice vibrated with despair and frustration.

Fourteen months ago his father had been involved in a car accident that had broken his right leg and pelvis. He'd been in the hospital for weeks, followed by months of painful rehab. Reid had given up the lucrative private security work he'd been doing in Europe and flown home to help out. It had been a short-term arrangement to get his parents through a tough time before he took off again, but the slowness of his father's recovery had soon changed that plan. After a couple of months of cooling his heels in between helping out around the orchard, Reid had applied for a job at Bozeman Police Department, his old stomping ground, and resigned himself to hanging around for a while in order to take the pressure off his father's recovery.

Running the orchard had always been a part-time occupation for the Daltons, with Reid's grandfather and father both splitting their time between maintaining the trees and running a small law practice in Marietta, but that didn't mean it wasn't demanding work. Depending on the season, the trees needed pruning, spraying, fertilizing. And then there was harvest time…

The four hundred apple trees that made up Dalton Orchards were in the low-maintenance phase of the growing cycle at the moment, however; the fruit was barely budding on the trees. There was no reason for his father to be risking his health by climbing up and down ladders, even if he was worried about the outbreak of apple scab he'd been trying to eradicate for a few months now.

"I'll talk to him," Reid said.

"Fat lot of good that will do. You're both as bad as each other."

Reid eyed his mother. He wasn't sure what he'd done to earn himself a share of her bad mood, but he wisely chose to retreat rather than investigate further. She'd be over her crankiness by dinner time, no doubt.

He tracked his dad down to the barn, where he found him tinkering with the apple press, the contents of his tool box spilling across the dirt floor. At sixty-three, Ross Dalton still had a full head of salt and pepper hair and a face that was worn from too many hours in the sun. He'd lost weight since the accident, and his worn jeans hung from his hips, making him look as though he was wearing borrowed clothing.

"Don't want to hear it," he said as Reid approached.

"How do you know you don't want to hear it when you don't know what I'm going to say?"

"Did she tell you about the ladder?"

"Yep."

"Then I don't want to hear it."

"You could have waited for me to get home," Reid said mildly.

"I'm fine. You saw my last X-rays. Everything's solid."

"Your reflexes are shot. You know that." Not to mention his father was still trying to rebuild his strength after months of reduced activities. "If you slipped or the ladder fell, there's no way you're fast enough to do anything about it. But I'm not going to lecture you."

"What do you call this, then?" his father asked sourly.

"A conversation."

His father grunted in response, but his mouth curled up at the corners. They'd always got along well, which was a good thing, since Reid was an only child.

"How'd your game go?" his father asked.

"All right."

His father shot him a searching glance, obviously picking up on the heaviness in Reid's tone.

"Something happened on the way home," Reid said. He needed to decompress after breaking the news to Tara, and he knew his words wouldn't go any further. "The guys and I spotted Tara's fiancé leaving the motel up on the freeway."

"I take it he wasn't with Tara?" his father asked.

Reid shook his head.

There was a short silence as his father processed the news. "You told her yet?"

"Yeah."

"How'd she take it?"

Reid remembered the way she'd fumbled for the seat when he'd broken the news about Paige. She hadn't cried, though. Hadn't shed a single tear.

"She's pretty tough," he said.

"Still. She must be upset."

Reid glanced out the door of the barn, remembering the tense set of her shoulders as she left the salon. "Yeah."

"You tell her if she needs any legal advice, it's on the house, okay?"

His father had been forced to wind up his practice after the accident, but he still took on odd jobs for neighbors and friends.

"Thanks, I will."

Reid knew that Tara and Simon had been together for three years, but he had no idea how complicated their financial arrangements were. He frowned as he thought about all the crap she was going to have to wade through. Moving Simon out of the house, canceling wedding plans, dealing with the inevitable gossip around town and at the station… all of that on top of the hours she already put in helping out her mother.

If he could make it all go away for her, he would. But he couldn't.

"I need a shower," he said, turning away.

He left his father to his tinkering, crossing to the wooden staircase that led to the self-contained apartment over the garage that had been his home for the past year.

Originally built to accommodate visitors from out of state—his mother came from a large family—the space was divided into sleeping, living and cooking zones, with a small bathroom. More than enough to accommodate his needs, and private enough that he didn't feel as though he was living in his parents' pockets.

That didn't mean he wasn't looking forward to having his own place again when he left Marietta. Which reminded him…

Crossing to the laptop he'd left on the coffee table, he called up his email program. There was nothing new, and he pushed the computer away. He'd interviewed for a job with a

Chicago-based security company over a month ago now, but they still hadn't gotten back to him.

The Klieg Security Group had offices in most states as well as an international arm, which meant there was plenty of scope for advancement and adventure for a guy who was looking for both. With his overseas security experience and police background, Reid was more than qualified to take on the role, and he was confident he had a good chance of landing it—if they ever got around to shortlisting candidates.

His thoughts shifted back to Tara. When he'd applied for the job, she'd been happily engaged, and the bright lights and challenges of a new role in a new city had held a lot of appeal. With his father coping well, there had been no reason for him to hang around in Marietta…

Don't even think it.

He was only human, however. And he'd been attracted to Tara from the moment he'd walked into the patrol bay at Bozeman PD and been introduced to his new colleagues.

She'd been filling out paperwork at a desk, dressed in her navy blues, her blonde hair neatly braided and pinned at the back of her head. She'd glanced up as he'd walked in with Sergeant Crawford, and he'd looked straight into her clear green eyes and felt the hot pull of instant attraction.

She'd stared back at him, an arrested, uncertain look on her face. Then she'd returned to her paperwork, a small frown creasing her forehead, and he'd known she felt it too.

He was so stupid, he'd been pissed when the Sergeant

had put them in the same car. Hadn't wanted to be distracted by his own instincts. But working with Tara—getting to know her—had been the best thing about the past year, hands down.

She was a great cop, conscientious and fair-minded. She was an even better person. Funny and tough, sweet and smart-mouthed. He'd laughed more with her than with any other woman.

And then Simon had proposed, and Reid had realized that it would probably be a good idea to think about moving on. He was overdue anyway, and his dad was getting stronger every day. Hence the job application, and the fact that pretty soon he might be packing his bags and moving on again.

He yanked his T-shirt over his head and tossed it at the laundry hamper. Only an asshole would see any advantage for himself in Tara's situation. She was heartbroken. The future she'd had planned for herself had just come crashing down around her. She wasn't suddenly going to turn to Reid, even if there had been that moment on that first day, and even if there had been other moments over the past year when he'd caught her looking at him or their hands had brushed or one of them had said something and that feeling—that connection—had shimmered in the air between them.

Men and women were attracted to each other all the time and didn't act on it. It didn't mean anything. And even if it did mean something, there were lots of reasons why he and Tara Buck were never going to be an item, not the least of which was the fact that he hadn't had a serious relationship with a woman since he'd broken up with Mary Kent before leaving Marietta six years ago. He moved around too much to do anything other than casual with women. And Tara was not casual. Not by a long shot.

The bottom line was that he was her friend, and that was all she needed him to be right now.

And so that was what he would be.

Chapter Three

TARA KNEW THAT Grant had spilled the beans the moment she entered the patrol bay the next morning. One second her fellow patrol officers were lounging around the open-plan workspace, leaning against desks, sucking in coffee and shooting the breeze before the morning briefing, the next they were stiff and self-conscious, their conversations stilted.

Half of them couldn't look her in the eye. The other half watched her with what she could only describe as fascinated pity.

Freaking awesome.

Reid pushed himself to his feet when he saw her, a frown on his face.

"Morning," she said tightly.

A few of the guys returned her greeting. Reid followed her into the briefing room as she made a beeline for the coffee machine.

"I didn't think you'd be in today," he said.

She could feel him watching her as she poured coffee into a mug. She was ridiculously proud of the fact that her hands remained steady.

"Life goes on, right?" she said, shrugging.

"Yeah, but it's not going to grind to a halt if you take a couple of days to get on top of things."

"What's to get on top of? He's gone, I had the locks changed. A few phone calls this afternoon and the wedding will be history."

She shrugged again, even though her shoulders felt stiff and unnatural.

"Tara. Come on. This is me," he said quietly.

She risked eye contact for the briefest of seconds. "Don't be nice to me, today, okay? Don't pussyfoot around or speak in hushed tones or worry I'm going to lose it. I'm fine. Today is just a day, like any other day."

She almost believed her own words. Almost.

She'd had to put eyedrops in this morning to take the redness from her eyes, and her back was sore from sleeping on the couch because even after changing the sheets she hadn't been able to lie down on the bed that had once been theirs.

But she was here, and she was going to do her job, and somehow she was going to get through this.

"Okay. If that's what you want," Reid said.

"It is."

"All right, people, let's get this show started." Sergeant Crawford's voice boomed around the room as he entered, the rest of the crew trailing in after him. The Sergeant's pale blue eyes lingered on Tara for a few seconds longer than strictly necessary and he gave her the smallest of nods.

Great, he knew as well. Was there a single person in the whole of the Bozeman PD who didn't know her private business?

Wrapping her hands around her coffee, she moved to the nearest chair and sat. Reid didn't follow her, but she was aware of him in her peripheral vision anyway, a tall, dark shape that she took great pains not to look at directly. She wouldn't be able to avoid him once they were on patrol, however. Hard to pretend someone wasn't there when they were just a few feet away.

Not for the first time she wished it had been someone else—anyone else, really—who had seen Simon and Paige leaving the motel yesterday. For some reason she couldn't explain, the fact that it was Reid, that he was the one who'd had to break the news to her, added an extra layer of humiliation to the whole situation.

She didn't want to appear pathetic in his eyes.

She forced herself to listen to the Sergeant's rundown of overnight incidents, but there was nothing ongoing for them to worry about and it wasn't long before the briefing was over.

Sergeant Crawford lingered, reading over some paperwork as everyone filed out. Reid waited for her near the door while she dumped her coffee down the sink. Her stomach wasn't particularly food-friendly at the moment; she'd poured the coffee more to have something warm to hang onto than anything else.

"Officer Buck, can I have a word before you head out, please?" Sergeant Crawford said.

Tara's gaze went to Reid, but he was already disappearing through the door with the last of the other guys, giving them privacy.

Bracing herself, she turned to her boss.

"Yes, sir?"

Sergeant Crawford hitched a thumb behind his belt buckle, a sure sign he was uncomfortable. In his late forties, he had thinning grey hair, narrow shoulders and a pronounced paunch.

"You know what this place is like—worse than a high school." He sounded almost apologetic. "We all know too much about each other's private lives."

"Yes, sir."

"If you need some space to sort yourself out, a week, two weeks, you've got time owing, and we can swing it for you. You only need to ask."

Tara shook her head immediately. "I appreciate the offer, but I'm fine. I want to work."

"It's your call."

She summoned up a tight smile. "Like I said, I appreciate the offer."

Reid was waiting for her in the patrol bay when she exited the briefing room, his gaze raking her face.

"All good?" he asked.

"Yep."

They walked out to the yard in silence. It was Reid's turn to drive, so she slid into the passenger seat. Reid started the engine before glancing at her.

"I know you don't want to talk about it, but my dad wants you to know that any legal advice you need is on the house."

She'd been sure she had no more tears left, but she felt the now-familiar hot sting at the back of her eyes at his words. She'd known the Daltons to nod at all her life, harvesting apples at the orchard every October being something of a tradition in her family, but since she'd been partnered with Reid she'd come to know them properly and she liked them a great deal. Every time she trekked out to the orchard to hook up with Reid for one of their cross-country runs, his mother insisted on stuffing her silly with home-baked muffins and breads, while his father was always ready to discuss current events or town politics.

"Thank him for me, but I don't think there will be anything to worry about."

She and Simon rented the townhouse, and while both their names were on the lease, she doubted Simon would be pushing to stay there. They hadn't quite reached the joint back account stage, either, something Tara could only be profoundly grateful for.

Reid looked as though he wanted to say more, but he simply nodded before signaling and pulling out of the yard.

Her phone shrilled to life as he headed south. She pulled it from the slot on her utility belt and checked the screen. Her family and friends knew better than to call her when she was working and Tara's heart gave a panicky squeeze when she saw her sister's name on the screen. Ever since her mother's diagnosis with Parkinson's disease, unexpected phone calls freaked her out. She wasn't sure what she was worried about—Parkinson's was a slow-moving disease, after all—but it didn't stop her heart from speeding up as she took the call.

"What's wrong?" she asked. "Is Mom all right?"

"Mom is fine, mostly because you haven't spoken to her yet, I gather." Scarlett's tone was bone dry.

"I figured there was no rush." Also, Tara hadn't been up to handling her mother's histrionics last night.

And there would be histrionics when she told her mother her news. Tammy Buck did not do calm, never had.

"Why are you at work?" Scarlett asked.

"Because I'm on the duty roster."

"Tara… for God's sake. You're allowed to have a few seconds of weakness, okay? The universe gives you permission to get a little sloppy when the man you were going to marry turns out to be a jerk."

Her sister's voice was loud enough that Reid must also be able to hear what she was saying.

"I'm not made of sugar. Why does everyone think I'm going to fall apart?"

First Reid, then the Sergeant, now her sister.

"Because your heart's just been broken, you idiot."

"We're on patrol, I can't talk now. I'll call you later."

She ended the call. Reid flicked a look at her. She waited for him to say something—anything—but the radio crackled to life, breaking the silence.

"118, 404…"

Tara grabbed her radio. Never had she been so happy to hear her badge number. "118, go ahead."

"118, respond to corner Durston and 19th for a two vehicle non-injury MVA."

"118 copy," Tara said.

Reid was already stepping on the gas and weaving more aggressively through the traffic.

Two hours flew by as they controlled the scene, took witness statements and directed traffic around the cleanup operation. They had a shoplifter to deal with next, then a traffic stop for a car with broken rear tail lights.

Throughout, Tara was aware of Reid's quiet concern. He didn't say anything—he'd said he wouldn't, after all, and Reid always kept his word—but she could feel how careful he was being around her. How sorry he felt for her.

Poor Tara, betrayed by her fiancé. Heartbroken and abandoned and humiliated.

The rational part of her brain reminded her that he was

her partner and friend—of course he was concerned for her. He was a nice guy. He was simply looking out for her.

It didn't stop her from grinding her teeth in frustration, and it didn't relieve the burning self-consciousness she felt every time she turned her head and caught him watching her.

She didn't want his sympathy, and she definitely didn't want his pity. What she wanted was to forget. She wanted to give herself over to the job and to simply push all the ugliness that had been bouncing around inside her for the past twenty-four hours into a dark corner and work.

Standing in the open patrol car door, she eyed her partner darkly, watching as he talked to the car owner about the damage to his tail lights. Some of the guys looked goofy in their navy blues, especially the ones who had let themselves get thick around the middle with age, but Reid wasn't carrying an ounce of extra fat anywhere on his tall, broad-shouldered body. He made the uniform look good, and more than one woman gave him a lingering glance as they passed by.

The driver said something, and Reid smiled, his eyes lighting up, making his handsome face even more attractive. Tara looked away, aware of a sudden, terrible urge to march up to him and shove him hard in the chest like a child in the school ground.

No point being angry with Reid. *You picked Simon. You agreed to marry the guy.*

She did, and she had. Focusing her anger on Reid, resenting his concern for her, was immature and a little crazy. She needed to get a grip.

She turned away so she didn't have to look at him, but the lump of hot anger sitting in her belly didn't go anywhere. Suddenly the need to cry was on her again. Her life was a mess—and the worst thing was, she'd played a part in making it that way.

The radio crackled, saving her from herself, and she leaned in to the car so she could hear it more clearly.

"404 to all units, we have a report of a theft of a motor vehicle in progress with a baby inside near the Post Office on Main."

Tara ducked her head out of the car. "Reid, we're up."

He glanced her way, giving her a sharp nod, and she slid into the passenger seat and reached for her radio.

"404, 118. We are in the area and we are responding."

Dispatch acknowledged her call, relaying the license plate details of a blue Ford sedan and letting her know that the car was last seen traveling west on Main. Reid slid into the driver's seat, slamming the door shut and starting the engine in one smooth move.

"What have we got?"

"Head west on Main. We're looking for a stolen Ford with a baby inside."

Reid swore quietly. All cops hated incidents like this, especially in summer. No thief set out to steal a car with a baby on board. Most of the time, they realized their mistake almost immediately, leading them to dump the car as quickly as possible. If they dumped it somewhere out of the way, however, the baby could potentially be left in the car for hours before it was found. On a hot June day like today, it didn't take long for a child to become dangerously dehydrated and overheated.

They cruised the area, both her and Reid scanning the passing traffic and side streets, looking for the blue Ford. She checked in with dispatch regularly, and they broadened their search area as other cars reported in.

She was about to report a clean sweep of the area near the Northgate Shopping Center when she spotted a flash of blue out of the corner of her eye. Sure enough, a bright blue Ford was traveling east along a side street. She craned her neck in order to see the license plate.

"Got him," she said, relief flooding her.

Reid's head snapped around, his gaze zeroing in on the car. Tara was already on the radio, calling it in and requesting emergency traffic only over the radio until they could pull off a high risk traffic stop. Dispatch confirmed, informing them that another car was on its way, then the radio began to emit the regular beeps designed to remind officers to use the radio only if absolutely necessary.

They trailed the car as discreetly as possible, not wanting to panic the driver. Once Wadley and Hayes had radioed to let them know they were in position, Reid flicked both lights and siren on.

Tara flashed a glance at him, taking in his intent expression and steady hands on the wheel. Reid was renowned for keeping a cool head in a crisis, one of the many reasons the other officers often deferred to him around the station. That and the fact that he was a natural leader. If he hadn't left the force six years ago and taken off overseas to do private security work, the odds were good he'd be well up the food chain by now.

The Ford sped up, swerving through an intersection and almost taking out an SUV. Reid followed with a smooth surge of power. Up ahead, blue lights flashed as Wadley and Hayes blocked the road with their car. It only took the thief a moment to understand he was trapped. The Ford swerved off the road, tires screeching before the car bottomed out on the curb with a resounding metallic crash. The car plowed into the side of the store on the corner and smashed to a halt. The door popped open almost instantly and a slim, dark-clothed figure slipped out of the car and bolted up the adjacent alleyway. A kid or a woman, Tara guessed, judging by the build and stature.

"404, 118. Car has stopped, suspect has abandoned the car," Tara reported as Reid hit the brakes hard.

She braced one hand on the dash, the other already on the door handle. The moment the car ceased moving, she was out and racing for the Ford. One glance in the side window was enough to assure her that the baby was alive and well, his face red with exertion as he exercised his lungs.

"404, 118. Baby is alive and well. I repeat, the baby is alive and well. 118 in foot pursuit."

She spun away from the Ford, taking off up the alley after the suspect. Reid or the other officers would take care of the baby.

The thief was at the far end of the alley, running like hell. Tara put her head down and gave it her all. Her feet slapped the pavement, her lungs and legs burned, and for the first time all day she felt almost good as she channeled all her hurt, humiliation, and anger into the chase.

Suddenly catching this asshole wasn't just a professional duty but a personal mission.

Digging deep, she lengthened her stride, determined to close the distance.

Chapter Four

TARA TOOK OFF up the alleyway at a flat sprint, arms pumping as she gave pursuit. By the time Reid made it to the head of the alley she was halfway down, running hard. She'd done track and field at school and he knew from personal experience that she was fast, but he was pretty sure he'd never seen her move like this.

"124 in foot pursuit," he told the radio, taking off after Tara and the suspect.

By the time he got to the end of the alley, he was just in time to see Tara disappearing down a cross street. Sucking in air, he pounded after her, not wanting her to come up against a desperate criminal on her own. She could take care of herself, he knew, but that didn't mean he liked the idea of her having to wrangle a freaked-out car thief single-handedly. The odds were good there were drugs involved, too, this sort of spontaneous, opportunistic car theft being typical of strung-out addicts.

He kept Tara in sight as he dodged his way down the street, sidestepping pedestrians and other obstacles. A part of him couldn't help but admire her smooth, even gait as she gained on the thief. She was like a gazelle when she ran—elegant, born to it, her narrow hips and long legs built for speed.

Suddenly she veered to the left, disappearing, and Reid was so distracted he almost went tumbling, smashing into an A-frame sign a store owner had placed on the sidewalk.

Shit.

He recovered quickly, once again building speed, streaking around the corner into yet another alleyway. He saw immediately that the far end was blocked by a chain link fence, the top covered with coils of razor-wire. The suspect had just reached it, springing up the chain link like a monkey, hands and feet clawing for traction. Tara was only seconds behind him, and as Reid watched she leaped at the fence, momentum giving her wings as she snatched at the suspect's back. She grabbed the guy's T-shirt, yanking backwards, and the two of them fell to the ground. Tara immediately rolled to her feet, while the suspect stayed low, scrambling toward the fence once again.

Reid was close enough now to see that the suspect was a woman, her face sunken and sallow, hair greasy, eyes bloodshot and wild. Meth user, he guessed, which meant she could be anything from plain old fashioned desperate to out-of-her-mind psychotic.

The woman barely had a grip on the fence before Tara was on her again, wrenching her backward.

"Police! You're under arrest." Tara's words echoed up the alley, strong despite the fact she was breathing hard.

The woman struggled, striking out at Tara. Tara's head jerked backward as a blow connected. Reid's lungs were on fire as he covered the final twenty feet, adrenaline lighting up every cell in his body, the need to get in there and control the situation and protect Tara a primal, undeniable urge.

Tara used her body weight against her assailant, rushing forward and pushing the other woman off balance. For a second the two of them hung suspended. Then they were both on the ground, Tara attempting to control the other woman by throwing her leg across her body. The woman struggled to throw Tara off, but Tara grabbed her right arm, twisting it up her back.

"You have the right to remain silent," Tara panted. "Anything you say can and will be used against you in a court of law. You have the right to consult an attorney…"

Reid slipped his cuffs from his utility belt, dropping to his knees the second he reached the two women. Tara leaned to the side without him having to say a word, allowing him to slip on the first cuff, and within seconds he had the woman's other arm cuffed tightly behind her back. Then and only then did Tara let up, taking her weight off the other woman's body.

"Fucking cop. Fucking broke my arm. I'm going to sue your ass off," the woman screamed, head thrashing from side to side, body bucking.

"You okay?" Reid asked, glancing at Tara.

"Of course."

Her hair had come loose during the struggle, and strands hung around her face. When she turned her head to look at him, he saw a cut and the beginnings of a bruise on her cheekbone.

"That hurt?" he asked, gesturing at her cheek.

Tara lifted a hand, touching her face, looking surprised when it came away with blood on it.

"I want a lawyer. I know my rights. You can't manhandle me like this," the other woman protested.

Tara stood, adjusting her utility belt. "Come on, on your feet."

She reached down and used her grip on the woman's wrists to force her first to her knees, then her feet. Reid called in to dispatch, letting them know they had the suspect in custody before relaying their position. His gaze kept going to the wound on Tara's face. It had been a good takedown, and she was okay, but he hated it that she'd been hurt.

"My arm hurts. I need a doctor, you bitch," the woman said.

"My name is Patrol Officer Buck, and you can request a medical evaluation when we take you in," Tara said.

Her tone was cold and hard, devoid of the professional distance she usually employed. Reid shot her a quick look, registering the stony expression on her face.

"Fuck you, Patrol Officer Bitch," the other woman said.

Her expression contemptuous, she spat in Tara's face.

Tara moved so fast, he almost didn't see her, reaching out to grab the woman's T-shirt in her fist, getting right up in her face.

"You want to try that again, you piece of crap?" Reid didn't recognize Tara's voice, it was so low and hard and dangerous. She shook the other woman, making her head rock on her neck.

"Tara," Reid said.

She didn't seem to hear him, her whole being focused on the thief. He reached out, grabbing her shoulder. He could feel how wound up she was, her body vibrating with suppressed emotion.

"I've got this," he said firmly.

She glanced at him, and for a split second her gaze was utterly blank, as though she didn't recognize him. And then she blinked and he saw awareness rush back in. Her shoulders dropped and she released her grip on the other woman so abruptly the woman staggered, off balance.

Reid concentrated on Tara, aware of the sound of sirens as their colleagues raced to join them.

"Tara?"

She turned her back on him.

"Talk to me, Tara."

Verbal abuse and physical assaults were part and parcel of the job, but he'd never seen Tara react like this before, not in all the months they'd been working together.

She took a deep breath, her shoulders lifting and falling with the force of it. Then she pushed the loose strands of hair back from her forehead and turned to face him.

"I'm sorry."

Her green eyes were clouded, troubled, and she looked close to tears. His gut impulse was to pull her into his arms, but they had a pissed-off meth user to take care of and a patrol car was going to join them any second.

"Go flag the others down," he said.

It was an unnecessary task, but he could see she needed a few seconds to pull herself together. She nodded and started walking to the top of the alley.

"Good riddance, bitch," the other woman yelled after her.

Reid spared her an irritated glance. On another day, he'd probably find some sympathy for the track marks on her arms and the open sores on her face, but not today.

Today, his thoughts were all for the woman walking away from him, and his inability to take her pain away.

TARA COULDN'T STOP her hands from shaking. She had to clasp them together behind her back to hide the fact while the suspect was read her rights again and helped into the backseat of a patrol car. Tara stood at a distance and kept her head down the whole time, avoiding eye contact with her colleagues. Especially Reid.

If he hadn't stepped in, she had no idea what might have happened. That was the ugly truth of it. She'd been so bound up in the moment, filled with an almost ungovernable anger… she could still feel the purity of it, the way it had burned its way through her body.

Insults often flew thick and fast when people were being called to account for their wrongdoings, but in five years on the job, Tara had never let them get to her. For a few minutes back there, though, she'd been so close to doing something irrevocable. Something that would have changed who she was as a person and a cop.

Shame burned a hole in her gut as she went over and over the scene in her mind. Would she have hit the other woman if Reid hadn't stepped in? A woman who was cuffed and helpless, unable to defend herself? She wanted to believe she wouldn't have—needed to believe it—but she honestly didn't know. In that moment, she'd been so angry, the rage boiling up from some hidden place within her.

"Come on."

Reid's hand landed in the small of her back for the briefest of moments as he encouraged her to walk alongside him. She matched her pace to his, her gaze fixed on the sidewalk.

"Everyone has bad days, Tara," he said after a minute. "Everyone loses it on occasion. You're only human, and if ever it was going to happen, today was probably the day, right?"

Reid's tone was so understanding, so matter of fact and

reasonable. She wanted to believe him, to let herself off the hook, but she'd never gone easy on herself.

"Have you? Lost it like that, I mean?" she asked.

She glanced at him, found him watching her.

"Of course. I'm not a saint. And neither are you."

Some of the tightness left her chest. Not all, but some.

"I always promised myself I was going to be a good cop. Take care of people, do the right thing."

"You are a good cop."

There was no arguing with his statement, he said it so unequivocally.

"I shouldn't have come into work today," she admitted.

He didn't say anything, one of the many reasons she liked him so much.

She could see the patrol car ahead. Someone had put out traffic cones to cordon off the scene. An ambulance crew stood with a woman who was holding the baby, her face still wet from tears. Normally Tara liked this part of the job, the bit where she got to interact with people who'd had good news, a good outcome. She was still feeling shaken and raw, however, and she hung back when Reid stepped forward to check that the mother was okay. She had to force a smile when the woman insisted on coming over so she could thank Tara personally for her efforts.

"I'll never forget this day, and how great you all were," she said, her blue eyes wide with sincerity.

"We're just glad the baby's okay," Tara said.

It was a relief to be in the car, driving back to headquarters. Tara flipped down the visor to check her face, touching the cut on her cheekbone tentatively.

"Should heal okay," she said, flipping it back up.

It was hard to get too worried about a bruise and a superficial cut when there were so many other things wrong with her life.

"You need to learn to duck."

"You need to learn to run faster."

He shot her a dry look and she almost smiled. She was fast, but in a neck-and-neck race they both know he'd beat her.

They pulled into the yard and parked the car. A couple of the guys called out congratulations as they headed inside. Tara was just pleased they had something to think about other than her personal life.

She caught Reid's elbow as they approached the patrol bay, stopping him so they could talk in the relative privacy of the corridor.

"So you know, I'm going to ask Sarge for a week off."

"Good."

He surprised her then by reaching out and brushing his thumb across her cheek, careful not to touch her cut.

"You should get this looked at, too. Just in case."

The contact was fleeting, less than the time it would take a person to blink, but the warmth of his touch stayed with her after he'd turned away. She stared at his retreating back for a long beat.

Then she took a deep breath and went to talk to the Sergeant.

SERGEANT CRAWFORD INSISTED she take two weeks' leave instead of the one she'd requested. She, in turn, insisted she would finish her shift rather than head home immediately. Consequently it was after five by the time she was back in Marietta.

She headed straight for her mother's place. Over the past few months she'd gotten into the habit of dropping in on Tammy every few days so she could take care of any little chores that needed doing—washing, vacuuming, cleaning up the kitchen. Her mother's Parkinson's disease was not yet so advanced that she couldn't still do these things for herself, but she had been struggling with mood changes and depression since her diagnosis, something the doctor was still trying to sort out with medication, and she tended to let things slide if Tara wasn't there to help her out.

And, of course, Tara needed to tell her mother what had happened with Simon.

She took a minute to compose herself when she arrived, listening to the car tick-tick as it cooled, preparing herself for her mother's reaction. Then she drew in a deep breath, let it out, and climbed out of her car.

"There you are. I was beginning to think I wouldn't see

you," Tammy said as Tara let herself in the front door.

Her mother was in her favorite chair by the window, a magazine in her lap. Her blonde hair was piled high and sprayed into place, her face perfectly made up, even though she probably hadn't left the house all day. She was wearing a pair of the tight black pants she favored, along with a leopard-skin T-shirt with a bejeweled neckline. The two-inch wedge-heeled mules she usually wore around the house—her idea of a casual shoe—sat beside her chair, at the ready in case someone who wasn't family came to the door.

Tara spared the damned things a dark look. Her mother wasn't supposed to wear high heels any more, her balance having been affected by the Parkinson's, but she insisted that she couldn't stand flat-heeled shoes and that she was too used to wearing heels to stop now.

"I had a few things to sort out at work," Tara said. "How have you been?"

She kissed her mother's cheek, breathing in the smell of hair-spray and Tammy's strong floral perfume.

"Oh, you know. The usual." Her mother shrugged, her mouth pulling down at the corners.

"Do you need me to get any groceries for you?" Tara said. Her stomach was tight. She so didn't want to do this.

"You took care of that last time, remember?" her mother said, giving her a curious look.

"Right." She'd cooked up some meals, too, and frozen them in portions for her mother. "Anything else that needs doing?"

"The bathroom could do with a once-over, if you wouldn't mind."

"Sure. Do you want me to take something out for your dinner?"

"If you like. I haven't been very hungry lately." Her mother attempted a wan smile.

"Well, you need to keep eating. You know that."

"I know."

Tara went into the kitchen and opened the freezer. Half a dozen plastic containers filled the basket, each neatly labeled in her own hand-writing.

"Chicken hotpot or chili con carne?" she called out.

"The chicken sounds good, thank you."

Tara pulled a container from the freezer's depths and left it on the counter. Her gaze went to the cupboard under the sink where the cleaning supplies were stored. It was so tempting to slope off to the bathroom and busy herself with cleaning rather than bite the bullet and do what needed to be done. But delaying wasn't going to make this task any easier.

"Would you like a cup of tea? Margot dropped in with some of that fancy Lady Grey stuff she gets online from France," her mother said from the kitchen doorway.

Without waiting for Tara to answer, she crossed to the counter with the slow, rigid gait that had been one of the first symptoms of her condition. She reached out to flick on the kettle, her hand trembling uncontrollably.

"Mom, there's something I need to tell you."

"Well, go ahead, then. No one's stopping you," her mother said with some of her old sass.

"Simon's been cheating on me. We broke up last night, and the wedding is off."

Her mother's eyes widened. A hand lifted to her chest, pressing flat against her sternum. "Oh. Tara. No. No, no, no." The last words came out on a wail. "This can't be happening. Not again. Tell me it's a mistake. Tell me someone got something wrong. You two are so good together. He's such a sweet man. So reliable and hard working."

"Reid saw him leaving a motel with the girl."

"Girl?"

"She's one of his students."

Her mother's mouth opened, but no sound came out. Tears were rolling down her face now, and the hand pressed to her chest clenched into a fist.

"No. I refuse to accept it. I won't accept it. I simply won't."

"I'm okay, Mom," she said, even though her mother hadn't quite got around to asking.

But her mother was already lost in a world of her own pain.

"Oh, Tara. I can't bear it. This is the one thing I wanted to protect my daughters from. The one thing. People talking and looking sideways at you in the supermarket. Everyone feeling sorry for you. And knowing that they're out there somewhere together, enjoying the happiness they stole from you. Laughing at you. Making up stories for each other to excuse their own weakness."

Her mother was shaking all over now, an emotional reaction and not a Parkinson's symptom.

"This can't be happening. It just can't. I won't let it. Do you hear me, I won't let it?"

The kitchen echoed with the high pitch of her mother's voice, every second word punctuated with a thump of her fist to her sternum.

"Mom, you need to calm down. Simon's not worth this kind of upset."

Her mother moved closer, reaching out to catch both of Tara's hands in hers. Looking into Tammy's faded blue eyes, Tara could see her bone-deep pain, still as fresh today as it had been thirteen years ago. She'd given everything to Jason Buck, and he had left her half a woman when he'd abandoned her. Her mother had never recovered. Worse, Tara suspected she didn't want to, that at a certain point, whether consciously or unconsciously, Tammy had decided that if the hurt her ex-husband had inflicted on her was all she had left, she would cleave to it utterly.

That was how much she'd loved her husband, how devoted she'd been to him.

"You can't hide your hurt from me, Tara. I know how hollow you feel right now. You loved that man, and he's taken all your happiness and trust and left you with nothing.

You will never be the same. Never."

No.

The single word came from a place deep inside Tara, an absolute denial of her mother's assessment of the situation. She'd planned a future with Simon, but she hadn't made him her everything. She'd never given a man that kind of power over her life and happiness. She might feel foolish, she might be embarrassed, but she wasn't broken. She wasn't shattered.

She frowned, trying to grasp the realization she sensed hovering just out of reach. Then that moment in the corridor at work today came back to her—Reid's thumb brushing her cheekbone, the heat from the small contact ricocheting through her body long after he'd gone—and something shifted inside her. Blinking stupidly, she suddenly understood something she'd never allowed herself to acknowledge before.

She had never loved Simon the way a woman should love her husband. He had never set her world on fire or consumed her thoughts. He had been good and steady. He had been attentive and kind. A good choice, in other words, for a woman bent on not repeating her mother's mistakes.

"Mom, you'll make yourself sick," Tara said, urging her mother toward the kitchen table so she could take a seat.

Inside, she was reeling as the full repercussions of her epiphany hit home: she'd almost married a man she didn't love.

"I'll take her. Why don't you see if she's got any of her tablets left?" Scarlett said from the doorway.

Tara had been so distracted, she hadn't heard the front door or her sister's footsteps in the hall. Scarlett edged Tara out of the way, giving Tara a sympathetic look before guiding their mother into a chair. Tara seized the reprieve her sister had offered and escaped to the hallway, walking briskly to her mother's bedroom.

She sank onto the end of the bed, feeling a little as though someone had sneaked up behind her and smacked her on the head with a two-by-four. She'd felt foolish yesterday when Reid had told her what he'd seen, but that was nothing compared to the searing sense of her own stupidity she was experiencing right now.

She'd made a deal with the devil, trading off love and passion for security and dependability—and then her stable, safe husband-to-be had cheated on her with a seventeen-year-old.

Her mother's voice floated down the hallway, tinged with hysteria, and Tara pushed herself to her feet. There would be plenty of time for self-recrimination later. Right now, she had her mother to deal with.

Chapter Five

It was past ten that night when Tara opened the door to her sister.

"Well. That was a barrel of laughs," Scarlett said. "Finally got Mom to go to bed. A minor freaking miracle."

At her sister's insistence, Tara had left her sister to finish the Herculean task of calming their mother. Scarlett had argued that with Mitch away, settling his affairs in Australia so he could move permanently to Montana, she had plenty of time on her hands, and Tara had let herself be talked out the door. There was only so much a person could handle, and Tara recognized that she had already pushed the envelope once today.

Now, Scarlett brushed past her as she entered the house, stopping in her tracks when she saw the packing boxes piled all over the living room.

"Don't tell me you're moving out?" Scarlett couldn't look more aghast if she tried. "He's the rat, Tara. He's the one who goes, not you."

"Relax. I'm just packing his stuff." As well as anything

that reminded her of him. Which, it turned out, was quite a bit.

"Oh. That's all right, then. Do you need a hand with anything?"

"Sure. Grab a box. Shove some stuff in it. Join the party."

Scarlett gave her a narrow-eyed look. "Have you been drinking?"

"Maybe." She'd needed it after her epiphany.

"Thank God. Hit me with whatever you're having."

Tara led the way into the kitchen, pulling down two glasses and pouring vodka shots for both of them. Scarlet gave her a look.

"You been drinking out of the bottle up until now?"

"Yep."

Tara was well aware that her younger-by-five-minutes sister considered her to be a stick-in-the-mud goody-two-shoes. Scarlett looked as though she couldn't decide whether to be impressed or appalled by the fact that she'd caught her sister drinking hard liquor straight from the bottle.

Tara knocked her shot back, hissing as the alcohol burned its way down. Scarlett followed suit, shaking her head.

"Yow. Okay, that should take the edge off."

Tara walked back into the living room and resumed stacking Simon's books into a box.

"Has he called?" Scarlett asked.

"Five times."

"Did you speak to him?"

"No, ma'am, I did not."

"Good. Have you spoken to the school yet?"

"Why would I do that?" Tara asked, frowning at her sister.

"Because he's screwing one of his students. He needs to lose his job."

Tara smiled grimly. "I think you're forgetting we live in a town with a population of ten thousand people. I guarantee that the school principal knew about Simon's extra-curricular activities about five seconds after I did."

"Good point. So he'll be out of a job first thing tomorrow morning."

"I'm guessing he's already had a phone call telling him not to come in."

Simon's life was in the toilet, no question about it. His career was shot, his reputation ruined. Then there were Paige's parents…

"You know Paige's dad used to be a pro football player?" Tara said conversationally. The vodka had set up a little heat factory in her belly, sending warmth radiating through her body.

"You're kidding me."

"He played two seasons with the Patriots. Apparently they used to call him The House."

Scarlett pressed her fingers over her lips to try to hide her smile.

"And Paige's mother is the head of the local chapter of the NRA."

Scarlett laughed outright. "No shit."

"No shit."

Scarlett's smile faded as she studied Tara. "You must feel so goddamned betrayed and heartbroken."

Tara glanced down at the box full of Simon's books. "Well, one out of two isn't bad."

"What is that supposed to mean?" Scarlett asked.

Tara eyed her sister, then walked to the couch and dropped into the cushions. She needed to be sitting for this conversation, she was pretty sure.

"I didn't love Simon. At least, I didn't love Simon in the way you should probably love the person you're planning on spending the rest of your life with."

"What are you talking about? You and Simon were great together. You were glowing when he asked you to marry him." Scarlett was looking at her as though she had rocks in her head.

"He was safe." There was a bunch of other stuff she could say, but that was it in a nutshell, really.

Scarlett was frowning, looking confused. "Well, yeah. He's a school teacher. He loves history. Sometimes he wears white socks with jeans. But you loved him, Tara."

"As a friend. As a person that I liked spending time with. But he didn't make me breathless. He didn't make all the little hairs on my arms stand on end sometimes, just because he walked into the room. I didn't dream about him. He was… a good choice. Solid."

Scarlett sat down beside her. "You really mean it."

Tara nodded. It had taken her most of the evening to sift through her own feelings and responses after her moment of clarity at her mother's house. For instance, she now understood that the anger she'd had so much trouble bottling up today had been all for herself, because she had very deliberately played it safe and picked a man who had Good Husband stamped all over him in an attempt to ensure her marriage would go the distance, and life had blown a big fat raspberry at her.

If you stepped back far enough and squinted, the irony of it all was kind of funny—especially if you'd had enough vodka. It was also really, really unfair. She'd been prepared to sacrifice a lot of things in order to secure her future happiness.

She'd been prepared to ignore the way she felt when Reid looked at her or touched her. She'd resigned herself to always wondering, never knowing. She'd accepted warmth and friendship instead of the intensity she'd witnessed between Scarlett and her new husband, Mitch, when he'd flown into town from Australia a few months ago and swept Scarlett off her feet and all the way to the altar.

And for what? Simon had betrayed and humiliated her anyway. She'd sacrificed all the good in an attempt to avoid the bad and gotten the bad anyway, regardless.

"I don't know what to say," Scarlett said, breaking the silence. "No, actually, that's not true. I do know what to say—I'm glad. I'm glad that dirty cradle-robber didn't break your heart, and I'm glad that you aren't going to spend the rest of your life married to someone you don't love."

Tara studied the pale mark on her finger, the only sign she'd ever worn an engagement ring. "I'm not quite at the glad stage yet. But I can almost see it, on the horizon."

"It doesn't mean Simon isn't a complete asshole," Scarlett said.

"Oh, he's definitely an asshole." An asshole with no self-control or ethics, and dubious values.

An asshole who had made it necessary for her to make an appointment for an STD check first thing tomorrow morning.

"Tara..." Scarlett reached out and took her hand. "What happened with Mom and Dad... it sucked. But that doesn't mean we should spend the rest of our lives looking over our shoulders, worried the same thing is going to happen to us."

"You appreciate the irony of saying that when it already has happened to me, right?" Tara said.

"No, it hasn't. Mom adored Dad. He took a part of her with him when he left," Scarlett said quietly.

Tara stared at her sister for a long moment. Then she nodded.

"You're right. It's different." That was the realization

she'd had today, after all. The hurt she was feeling was nothing compared to her mother's, because her feelings hadn't been as deeply engaged.

"The truth is, life is a crapshoot," Scarlett said. "You can die choking on a peanut, or you can live to be a hundred." She shrugged. "No one knows. But you know what? I'm not gonna stop eating peanuts. I love Mitch more than I can say, and if something happens to him, or between us, I am going to be a hot mess for a long time. But I'm not going to give him up, either."

Her sister's words had the ring of absolute truth about them. Tara squeezed her sister's hand.

"You're braver than me," she admitted.

"No, I'm not. We're just brave in different ways. I would never have been able to make myself marry Simon, for example. Not for all the security in Fort Knox."

"I would never have taken off for the other side of the world to marry a man I'd met on the internet," Tara said.

Scarlett rolled her eyes. "And look how well that turned out."

"You still did it. There are so many things I have never done because I was too scared or I thought it wouldn't look good or some other stupid, dumb reason."

"Like what?" Scarlett asked.

Tara thought for a moment. "I've never traveled."

"Easily fixed. Next."

"I always wanted a motorbike."

Scarlett's jaw dropped. "Shut the front door."

Tara nodded. "Not a Harley Hog or anything huge. It looks like fun, you know?"

"What else? No, wait!"

Scarlett scrambled to her feet and rushed into the kitchen. When she came back she was carrying the bottle of vodka and a pad and pen.

"We should make a list, so you don't forget any of this stuff. A bucket list."

"I'm twenty-six."

"Okay, a fuck-it list, then."

They both laughed. For the first time in days, Tara felt okay. Not happy—it was going to be a while before she could forgive herself for the mistakes and decisions she'd made—but okay.

"Item number one: a new haircut," Scarlett said, pretending to write it down.

Tara shoved her sister in the shoulder. "Nice try. Put the motorbike at the top of the list."

Scarlett grinned and did so. "What next?"

Tara gazed off into the distance. There were so many things…

"I want to have a reckless, wild affair with a man I can't say no to," she said, the words popping out of her mouth without her even thinking about them.

"Better than the bike. Way better," Scarlett said, adding it to the list. "I'm putting it at the top."

Tara reached up to scratch her nose, hoping her face wasn't as red as it felt. Thank God her sister wasn't a mind reader, because she didn't want to have to explain why she'd had Reid's image in her head when those words had slipped out of her mouth.

"What next?" Scarlett asked, pen poised.

Tara reached for the vodka bottle. It was going to be a long list.

FIVE DAYS LATER, Reid shouldered the ladder and began the walk back to the house. They'd have to start netting soon, the fruit being at a point where birds would soon be interested in trying their luck, but the apple scab his father had been worried about appeared to have finally been vanquished. For now. The battle with Mother Nature was never truly over, and no side ever really won or lost. Growing up on the orchard had taught him that.

"Reid."

He looked up to see his mother making her way toward him, his phone in her hand.

"Hey. I was just coming in now," he said.

This was his first day off all week, and he'd spent the bulk of it in the orchard, taking care of all the little jobs his father wasn't quite up to tackling.

"Your phone made a noise. I knew you've been expecting something, so…" His mother passed the phone over.

Reid set down the ladder. "It's probably just one of the guys."

But when he opened the email, the first thing he saw was the Klieg Security Group logo.

"Well?" his mother asked.

"It's from Klieg."

"And?"

He scanned the email. "I've been shortlisted. They want me to go back for another interview."

"I knew it. Congratulations." His mother rested her hand on his shoulder as she leaned in to give him a kiss.

She was smiling, but her eyes were sad as she released him.

"Did they say when they might want you to start?"

"I think all of that's up for grabs," he said. "If I get the job."

"They'd be crazy not to take you."

He slipped the phone into his pocket and hefted the ladder. They both began walking. His mother was uncharacteristically silent, and when he glanced across at her she looked pensive.

"Might as well spit it out, Mom," he said.

Because she clearly wanted to talk about something. His dad, probably. Although why she thought Reid's nagging would have any more affect than hers he didn't know.

"All right, smarty pants." She ran her hand over the top of her head, smoothing her dark, shoulder-length hair.

"Hank Dearborn called me yesterday. He wanted to talk to me about buying out the orchard."

Reid frowned. The Dearborn family had a smaller orchard a little further out of town, and last year they'd started bottling their own cider and marketing it locally.

"I thought Dad rejected an offer from them a few years ago?"

"He did. But things are different now, and I wanted to talk to you before I spoke to your father."

Reid stopped and let the ladder rest on the ground. This wasn't the kind of conversation you had on the run.

"He's going to say the same thing he said last time—no," Reid said.

"He might. Or he might see things the way I do. Neither of us is getting any younger, and since you're not interested in taking on this place, we need to think about the future. If we sell now, we won't have the pressure of it hanging over our heads. Your father can relax a little."

"Dad doesn't want to relax."

"Well, he needs to," his mother said, her tone a little sharp.

"Mom, what's he going to do? Sit around and read the paper all day? He's sixty-three."

"And he's got more metal in his leg and pelvis than that damned ladder you're holding. The fact is, we have to make this decision sometime, Reid, and it's never going to be easy."

Reid glanced up at the Macintosh apple tree spreading its branches over her head. His grandfather had planted it in 1954, along with the Granny Smiths. The Early Golds had come later, and the Cortlands were his father's additions. When he was ten, he'd planted a row of trees, too, and every time he was home he made a point of checking on them.

"We don't expect you to give up your dreams to live ours," his mother said. "But we can't hang onto this place just because it holds sentimental value for you. It's not a pocket watch, it's a dirty, great big orchard."

It was true, his parents had never so much as hinted that they were disappointed he hadn't followed the family tradition and studied law. He'd made it clear from his early teens that he wanted to travel, and they had encouraged him to do so and always been interested in what work he was doing and the places he'd seen. But he didn't believe for a second that they didn't care about the orchard, or that they wouldn't feel it if they had to let it go. Hell, he'd feel it, and he'd always resented the place.

The work he'd had to do before and after school. The fact that there was always something that needed to be done, and that the growth cycle of the orchard dictated so many aspects of their lives.

"I don't know what you want me to say."

"I want to know that you're not going to regret it if we sell," his mother said, her gaze very direct.

"I don't have a simple answer to that question," he said.

Because the truth was, he hadn't hated helping out this past year. In fact, a lot of the time he'd enjoyed it, working in the outdoors alongside his father. As a teenager, life had been elsewhere. As an adult, he appreciated the fresh air and sunshine, the simple straight forwardness of the work.

"I appreciate that, but I told Hank I'd get back to him soon, so we all need to think about this."

"Only because he's made an offer. In real terms, there's no reason why you couldn't hire people in to do some of the work once Dad doesn't feel up to it anymore," Reid said.

"We could, but it would just be putting off the inevitable."

She was right, but it didn't stop him from feeling a twinge of angry resentment that she was forcing him—them—to this decision point now, when it wasn't strictly necessary.

They walked in silence the rest of the way back to the house.

"Are you joining us for dinner?" his Mom asked when they reached the point where he needed to peel off toward the barn.

"Thanks, but I've got something to do," he said.

She caught his arm as he turned away. "I know you don't want to face this, Reid, but it's not something we can all just ignore. I'm not asking you to make the decision for us, but I am asking you to make it with us."

Reid stared after her as she headed into the main house.

One thing about his mom, she had always been great at nailing a person to the wall. She always called a spade a spade, and never bullshitted when the truth would do.

Tara was like that, too. Straight up and honest, even if it was sometimes to her own detriment.

Reid dumped the ladder against the barn wall, aware that his thoughts had once again drifted to Tara. She'd been in and out his head all week, even though he hadn't heard from her since she finished her shift on Sunday. Sergeant Crawford had given her two weeks off, and he'd been doing single-car patrols in her absence.

He'd missed her, though. She always had something to say, and usually it was funny or interesting or both. He missed her light touch, too. No one was better at defusing a tense situation; there was something about Tara's calm common sense that kept people grounded, himself included.

Most of all he missed the sense of having her nearby, and knowing that he had only to turn his head and she'd be there, ready with a pithy comment or a laugh or a smile.

Better get used to that. If you get that Klieg job, you'll see her once or twice a year, if that.

And when he did see her, she'd probably be with some new guy, because it wouldn't take long for some smart bastard to snap her up. She was gorgeous, she was hot, she was funny and smart.

Pretty much the perfect woman.

Jesus. Can you hear yourself? Next thing you know you'll

be writing bad poetry and singing beneath her bedroom window.

His dad had left the toolbox near the apple press, and he hefted it back to the workbench where it belonged, dusting his hands on the seat of his jeans when he was done.

It was fruitless to spend too much time brooding over Tara. He'd made that decision long ago. It wasn't just that she'd been in a relationship with Simon the entire time he'd known her—although that was definitely a contributing factor. Tara was a Marietta girl, through and through. She loved the town, the people, the weather. She was content here, saw her future here. More importantly, her family were here, too, and they meant the world to her.

Whereas he'd had itchy feet ever since he'd opened his first atlas and understood how big the world was.

Even if she hadn't been with Simon, that fundamental difference in their outlooks would have stopped him from making a move. He hadn't spent more than eighteen months in one spot since he'd left Marietta when he was twenty-four, and he was on the verge of moving on yet again. He might be powerfully attracted to Tara, but he liked her a hell of a lot, too, and the last thing he'd ever want to do is hurt her. She was a dream. A sweet, hot dream, but a dream nonetheless, and he needed to stop thinking about her.

Determined to put words into action, he headed up to the apartment and changed into his running gear. An hour later, he was sweaty and exhausted and more than a little hungry. He showered, then heated up the leftover spaghetti and meatballs he'd made last night, sitting in front of the TV to eat. The baseball game was on, and he cracked open a beer and settled in for a lazy evening.

The Cardinals were starting their second inning when his phone rang. He didn't recognize the number but took the call anyway.

"Dalton speaking."

"Reid. Thank God. I wasn't sure if this number was current or not. It's Scarlett calling, Tara's sister."

He leaned forward and set his beer on the coffee table. "Scarlett. What's up?"

"Straight to the point, just like Tara." Her laugh was a little nervous.

"I figured that you wouldn't go to the trouble of tracking down my number and calling for nothing."

"True. The thing is, I can't find Tara. I've tried her place, I've tried her phone. I wondered whether maybe she was with you…?"

"No."

She sighed. "Okay. Then I guess my next question is if there is some way you can put an alert out without it being a big deal? In case I'm just being a nervous nelly and freaking out over nothing."

"Her phone battery is probably just dead. Or she could be out with friends, or seeing a movie."

"You think I'm over-reacting, and normally I would totally agree with you. But she only picked up the motorbike the day before yesterday, and even though I know she's probably being super safe and careful, I can't help worrying."

He blinked. "Tara bought a motorbike?"

"On Wednesday. I wanted her to go for the blue one but she had to have red. It's a Suzuki Boulevard something or other. I keep forgetting the model number."

He was still stuck on the part where Tara handed over cold hard cash for a two-wheeled suicide machine. Between the two of them, they had attended enough road accidents to know how dangerous motorbikes were.

"Why in hell would she buy a bike?" he asked.

"It's a long story."

"Give me the short version."

"She's living a little. Catching up on things she let slide by."

There was a cautious note beneath Scarlett's voice, and Reid guessed he was only getting part of the story.

"So, is there something you can do? Someone you can call in the sheriff's department, maybe, who could just keep an eye out or let you know if there have been any accidents…?" Scarlett asked.

"Let me make a few calls, I'll get back to you."

He swore when he ended the call. What in the hell was Tara thinking? He dialed the sheriff's office, his mind full of horror images from accident sites. He had a quick word with Harrison Pearce, who was happy to inform him that there had been no road accidents involving motorbikes in the area. Then he called Scarlett back, determined to get more information this time.

"No accidents," he said when Scarlett took the call.

"Oh, thank God. Thank you so much for checking."

"When was the last time you spoke to her?"

"Lunchtime. She said she was going to go for a run, then maybe go out on the bike. I was thinking we could get takeout for dinner, but she hasn't answered any of my calls or returned my messages."

Which Reid knew from personal experience was unusual for Tara.

"She didn't say anything else? Mention anything else she might want to do or go?"

There was a pause and he could almost hear Scarlett thinking on the other end of the phone.

"The only other thing I can think of is that she said she wanted to try the mechanical bull at that place near the train line."

Reid was pretty sure he hadn't heard properly. "Did you just say mechanical bull?"

"That's right. What's the name of that bar on the north side of town, the one with the broken neon sign?"

"The Wolves Den."

He stood, unable to stay seated.

"That's the one. They've got a bull there, right?"

"I have no idea."

He hadn't hung out at the Den since he'd first started to drink. Unlike Grey's Saloon and some of the other places in town, the Den was all about getting hammered and it attracted an ugly crowd.

"Maybe I should go over there and check. Just to put my mind at ease," Scarlett said.

Reid had a vision of Scarlett walking through the door at the Den in her usual get-up of tight T-shirt and snug, hip-hugging jeans. There'd be drool on the bar within seconds, and the queue of guys who'd insist on buying her a drink would form to the left.

"Why don't I do a drive by, see what I can see?" he said.

"You don't have to do that."

Yeah, he did. There was no way he was going to be able to concentrate on a freaking baseball game with pictures of Tara fending off drunken idiots or sliding off her brand new motorbike bouncing around in his head.

"I'm heading over that way anyway," he lied. "I can duck my head in."

"Well, okay, then. Although I'm going to feel pretty stupid when it turns out she's gone into Bozeman to shop or something."

He'd much rather Scarlett feel foolish than any of the alternatives his imagination was throwing up. That was the problem with being a cop—he had seen too many bad things over the years.

He pulled on a pair of jeans, put on his boots and

shrugged into a T-shirt. Tucking his phone into the back pocket, he took the stairs two at a time. The GMC fired up with a dull roar and seconds later he was shooting up the driveway, gravel spurting beneath his tires. It was only a short drive into town, and he navigated his way from the well-lit center to the less-illuminated industrial sector north of the train line. The Den's neon sign had lost its N years ago, and the neon blue made everything seem gray as Reid turned into the parking lot. There were a handful of motorbikes parked near the stairs to the bar, but none of them were red Suzukis.

He pulled out his phone to call Scarlett, then hesitated when he caught sight of the roof of a black pickup tucked into the corner. Tara had a black pickup.

He cruised up the aisle until he could see the number plate.

Yep, Tara's.

Feeling like he'd slipped down the rabbit-hole, he parked the GMC and headed for the entrance.

Chapter Six

IF ANYONE HAD asked Reid, he would have said The Wolves Den was the last place he would ever find Tara Buck.

But apparently he was wrong.

It was a Friday night and the place was crowded, people standing three or four deep at the bar. The mechanical bull was on a raised platform in the rear corner and clearly visible from the front entrance. The rabbit-hole feeling intensified as he spotted a slim, athletic figure astride the bucking beast, her blond hair whipping back and forth in the air as the machine tried to toss her.

He mouthed a four letter word and started pushing his way through the crowd, his gaze glued to Tara's jerking, swaying body. If she came off…

The bull was becoming more and more belligerent, spinning wildly now, throwing her back and forth. Tara had one hand high in the air, the other white-knuckle tight on the strap—and she was laughing and whooping like a good old cowgirl.

A crowd had formed around the safety barrier, cheering her on. Mostly men, Reid noted sourly. And who could blame them? Tara's blue tank top clung to her breasts and torso, while well-worn denim hugged her thighs. She looked wild and a bit dangerous and a lot sexy as she rode the bull like a rodeo champion.

The bull slowed, only throwing out the odd flick here and there to set Tara swaying. Finally it stopped entirely, and the crowd let up an almighty roar as Tara punched the air.

"Goddamn, you did it, girl," a tall cowboy said, stepping forward and lifting her off the bull.

She was laughing, pushing her hair off her face, her eyes shining. Someone passed her a beer and she chugged half of it down before lifting it high in the air in a triumphant salute. When she lowered it, one of the guys stepped in to top her drink up from a pitcher, filling it to the brim.

Reid muscled his way to the front of the crowd.

"Tara."

Her head swung round. It took her a moment to register him, then her face split into a big, beaming smile.

"Hey! What are you doing here? You just missed my big ride. Four in a row, no falls," she said. "Everyone's telling me it's a new record."

"This girl can ride," the tall cowboy said.

Tara's hair was tangled around her shoulders, her tank top low-cut enough that he could see the shadowy valley between her breasts. She looked Playboy-bunny good—

pretty, sexy, fun.

And more than a little drunk, unless he missed his guess.

"Ready to go five for five, sweetheart?" a husky guy behind her asked.

The crowd cheered and Tara laughed.

"Sure. Why the hell not?" She chugged the rest of her beer, banging the empty glass down onto the tabletop.

"Whoa, whoa, whoa," Reid said, stepping forward and catching her upper arm. "Not so fast."

"What's wrong?"

Not wanting to embarrass her, Reid lowered his voice and leaned closer. "How much have you had to drink?"

She blinked, then laughed. "I don't know. Enough to feel good."

"What if you come off?"

"Haven't yet." Her smile was full of cocky confidence.

Reid considered his options—throw her over his shoulder and forcibly drag her out of the bar, or let her have her head.

"Walk a straight line for me," he said.

She frowned, tucking a strand of hair behind her ear. "What?"

"You heard me. Pass a field sobriety test for me and I'll let you climb on board."

"Let me? Good luck trying to stop me, buddy," she said, giving him a look. "You might not have noticed, but women got the right to vote about a hundred years ago."

He didn't say anything, just eyed her steadily.

"I'm not drunk," she said, chin coming up.

"Prove it to me."

Her eyes narrowed. Then she tossed her hair over her shoulder.

"Okay, fine. But if I pass the test, you're next on the bull."

He glanced at the piece of battered machinery over her shoulder. "If that's the way you want to play it."

"It's exactly the way I want to play it, Dalton."

She turned and waved a hand at the opportunists crowding around like starving men at a buffet. "Give me a bit of room, boys, while I prove Officer Dalton wrong."

A few eyebrows went up as his profession was noted and the crowd shuffled backward, clearing a patch roughly three foot by seven.

"Hope you've got a strong grip, because that bull bucks like crazy," Tara said.

"Let's see you stand on one leg first," he said.

Tara lifted one booted foot off the ground and eyeing him smugly.

"Good enough for you?"

No sooner had she spoken than she lost her balance, wavering wildly, arms flailing before catching herself.

Reid crossed his arms over his chest and cocked an eyebrow.

"I didn't fall," Tara said, stabbing a finger at him. "I did not touch my foot to the ground. I want that on the record."

The crowd stirred around them, a couple of people throwing in their two cents' worth.

"Walk and turn. You know the drill," he said, gesturing with his chin.

Tara contemplated the space that had been cleared, then started to walk, each foot placed very deliberately and directly in front of the other.

"Note the straight line," she called over her shoulder.

When she got to the end, she swiveled on her heel, just to show she could, he suspected. For the second time she nearly lost her balance, staggering slightly to the left.

"That wasn't fair," she said immediately. "Let me do that again."

"Too late. You failed, I win. Let's go home," he said.

"I want another test."

"Tough luck." He stepped forward to grasp her elbow.

Tara frowned. "I don't want to go home. I'm having a good time, and I'm doing new things and meeting new people."

Okay, she was definitely three sheets to the wind.

"Why don't we go grab a burger, maybe some coffee?" he suggested.

She pulled her arm free. "I'm riding the bull again, and you can't stop me."

She made a break for the bull, not unlike a child insisting on one last play on the swing set before leaving the park.

Reid swore under his breath and went after her.

Plan B it was, then.

Wrapping an arm around her middle, he pulled her back toward him. She squawked out a protest, twisting to face him, and he bent so that his shoulder was tucked against her belly, pulling her off balance at the same time. She toppled onto his shoulder, and he turned and immediately headed for the door, one arm banded across the back of her thighs to lock her in place. It took her a second to comprehend what he'd done, and when she did she started to wriggle and twist around, fists battering his back, doing her best to force him to release her.

He simply tightened his grip, his gaze on the distant exit, and kept walking.

The crowd parted, and seconds later he was outside, bending to set Tara back on her feet.

"I can't believe you just did that," she spluttered, her face red, her green eyes wide.

"Believe it. You want to grab something to eat before I take you home or not?"

She made a face to let him know she thought he was demented.

"No, Dalton, I do not want to grab a burger with you after you just rained on my parade like the biggest wet blanket of all time. What I'd like is for you to stop being the fun police and leave me to my awesome night out." She planted her hands on her hips, her chin tilted aggressively.

So drunk. A part of him wanted to laugh at her, but most of him just wanted to get her out of the seedy end of town.

"Answer me honestly—do you know a single person in that bar?"

"Sure. The tall guy is Jonah. The guy with the white hat is Drew. Or maybe Duncan… something with a D, anyway." She frowned as she tried to remember.

"And how many drinks do you think those good ol' boys have bought you since you've been here?" he asked.

"I'm not stupid, Reid. I can take care of myself."

There was a reckless, almost dangerous light in her eyes. He'd never seen her like this before, and he was pretty sure it wasn't just because she'd had a few too many.

"What's going on, Tara? Why are you hanging out at this dump? Why did I hear from your sister tonight that you bought a motorbike?"

"Because I did. And I love it."

Her chin ratcheted higher. He narrowed his eyes, trying to work out what was going on with her.

"Is this because of what Simon did? Are you trying to prove something to him or—"

"This is about me." She jabbed a thumb at her chest. "About who I am, and how much I've missed out on because I'm such a goody-two-shoes. I'm sick of always doing the right thing, Reid. I'm sick of being the one who always picks up the pieces. And I'm really sick of being so careful all the time."

She was trembling with the vehemence of her words, her shoulders thrown back as though she was declaring herself or claiming territory for her country. He thought about what he knew of her life—her scatterbrained, irresponsible twin, her melodramatic mom, the way she conducted herself at work, what he'd seen of her relationship with her ex—and he started to get an inkling of where she was coming from.

Because Tara was a good person. She always did the right thing, always stepped up, never said no. She worked hard, pitched in to help her mom out, dug her sister out of rough spots.

"Okay. I get that," he said. "But do you really think breaking your neck on a stupid bull is the right way to fix any of that?"

Tara took a step toward him, her expression fierce. "What do I care about the right way? Don't you get it? I don't want to be afraid any more. I don't want to worry about what people think or what might happen or when people will leave or if they'll stop loving me. I'm over it."

Tears flooded her eyes and her chin wobbled. Her jaw set, she lifted her gaze to the sky and blinked like crazy, trying to suck it all back in.

"It's okay," he said quietly.

He wasn't going to think any less of her for crying.

She shook her head. "No. I've cried enough. I'm done with it."

He wanted to put his arms around her so badly his shoulders ached. But they'd never had that kind of relationship and he figured now was probably a really bad time to start.

"Come on," he said. "Let me take you home."

For a moment he thought she was going to object, but after a short pause she nodded and fell into step beside him as he walked to his pickup. He held the door open for her and she climbed inside. He could feel her watching him as he rounded the front of the truck.

"I'm not taking the bike back," she said as he slid behind the wheel.

He held his hands in the air. "Like you said, I'm not the boss of you."

She sniffed, and he got the sense she was disappointed he hadn't offered her an argument.

"And I could have handled that bull, too. I'm a natural."

He started the truck and put it into gear. "Hip fucking hooray. I'll alert the Nobel Prize Committee."

There was a moment of shocked silence. Then Tara started laughing. The sound was so infectious, he couldn't help smiling as he pulled out of the parking lot and onto the road.

"I knew there was a reason I liked you," she said.

"Only one?"

"I wouldn't push my luck if I were you. I'm still getting over the fact that you just carried me out of a bar like a sack of potatoes."

"You weigh more than a sack of potatoes. For the record."

The corners of her mouth curled into a rueful smile. "You know what the sad thing is? That's the most charming thing you've said to me all night."

"I wasn't aiming for charming."

"You got that right."

The brightly-lit window of the Main Street Diner was coming up on his left. He glanced at her.

"Sure you don't want a coffee?"

"I'm thinking that I probably wouldn't mind a shower," she said, wrinkling her nose. "Is it just me, or do I smell like beer?"

"I wasn't going to say anything. But yeah, you do."

"Your honesty is so refreshing."

"Wish I could say the same for that beer stink."

She huffed out a little laugh. She was still smiling when he turned into the driveway of her townhouse development, driving past the other houses until he reached hers at the end, but her smile faded as he braked to a stop.

"I suppose I should thank you," she said grudgingly.

"You can call me tomorrow if you like, when you'll mean it."

She glanced out at the townhouse but didn't make a move to exit.

"I could have handled that bull."

"You're the expert."

"And you're a smart ass and a wet blanket."

"It was my pleasure."

Her smile was more fleeting this time, and he got it—she didn't want to go inside.

If he didn't care so much, if he didn't want her so much, he'd invite himself in for coffee, but he knew that wasn't a good idea.

"All right. Maybe I'll call you tomorrow and thank you, maybe I won't," she said, finally moving to open the car door.

The interior light came on, and he saw her face properly. She looked sad, and more than a little lost.

"What are you doing tomorrow?" he asked.

"Why?"

"Because I asked."

She studied him for a beat. "Nothing, I guess. Except for collecting my car."

"I'll pick you up at seven. Wear your swimsuit, and bring a change of clothes."

She blinked. "My swimsuit."

"Seven sharp. Don't keep me waiting."

She thought about it for a second, then she slid from the car. "I don't suppose there's any point asking what we'll be doing or where we'll be going?"

"Correct."

She shut the door, shooting him a look through the window to let him know she didn't think he was funny. He gave her a mock salute, then put the car into gear and backed out of the driveway.

When he reached the road and glanced back, the lights were on in her townhouse, the door safely shut.

He paused for a moment, thinking about what she'd said to him, what he'd seen. Then he headed for home. He had an early start tomorrow.

Chapter Seven

THE ELECTRONIC SCREECH of the alarm clock woke Tara at six-thirty, and she batted the damned thing off the bedside table in a futile attempt to silence it. It kept squealing from its new position on the floor near the foot of the bed, and she threw back the covers with a disgusted grunt.

Which was when she registered she was the proud owner of a throbbing headache, and that her right shoulder was inexplicably sore. Then last night came back to her and she realized that her sore shoulder was perfectly explicable, given that the mechanical bull had tried to rip it from its socket several times last night.

The clock was still nagging at her, so she crawled to the end of the bed and switched it off. She flopped back onto the mattress, lying on her belly, her sore arm hanging over the side of the bed, and wondered what Reid would do if she texted him and told him she'd changed her mind about their outing.

He'll just turn up anyway.

He would. He'd knock on the door and honk his horn

and bully her until she got dressed and went with him—wherever that might be—so she might as well suck it up and have a shower and try to choke down some breakfast.

The shower was good, the hot water easing some of the stiffness in her shoulder, but food wasn't something she could do, she decided. She'd never been a great drinker, but she'd had two hangovers in the space of a week—one from her vodka night with Scarlett, and today's doozy. Probably time to ease up on her alcohol consumption for the foreseeable future.

She swallowed a couple of painkillers and was just stuffing a towel and underwear into her backpack when she heard the rumble of Reid's truck.

She went to the door but hesitated a moment before opening it. She wasn't sure how she felt about last night, about what he'd done and the things she'd said to him. She definitely felt exposed—that was not up for debate—but she couldn't decide if she was annoyed with him for dragging her out of the bar or grateful or maybe even touched that he cared enough to do what he'd done in the first place.

But her feelings had always been complicated where he was concerned. From the moment he walked in the door at Bozeman PD, she'd been drawn to him. At first she'd told herself it was natural that she'd be curious about him after she'd heard the other guys talk about him so much. He'd only served as a Patrol Officer for four years before heading overseas to work in private security, but enough of the guys who'd trained and worked with him were still around that she'd heard plenty of stories about Reid Dalton.

Then they'd been on foot patrol during their first week of being partnered together, and he'd reached out to catch her when she'd stumbled over a crack in the sidewalk, and she'd been forced to admit that what she felt for him was more than simple curiosity. The echo of his touch had burned through her body, sending heat up into her face and down to places she hadn't wanted to think about, pushing her heart rate sky high, making her jumpy and self-conscious and hyper-aware of him.

She'd been living with Simon for a year by then, and it hadn't taken her long to rationalize the moment into a nice, safe little box. Reid was a good-looking guy, after all. Any woman would get a little hot under the collar if he grabbed her around the waist and saved her from an embarrassing face plant. He also had a dry, sometimes goofy sense of humor, was extremely well-read and well-traveled, and wasn't afraid to let the world know when he cared about something. All in all, a pretty appealing package, and she was only human. It didn't mean anything.

Amazing how long she'd been able to cling to that piece of self-delusion.

She heard Reid's heavy tread mounting the steps to her front door and pulled it open before he could knock. His hair was wet from the shower, making it appear almost black, and a long-sleeved black T-shirt and jeans made the most of his lean, strong body.

Pretty appealing package, my ass.

The man was gorgeous, that was the truth of it, but it was the kindness and intelligence behind his eyes that she'd always found the most appealing. God help her.

"You ready?" he asked.

"Two seconds," she said.

She turned on her heel and went to collect her wallet, house keys and phone. He was standing on the porch when she turned around. Watching her.

She'd gotten pretty good at reading his expressions over the past year. His eyebrows tended to lower a little when he was serious, and his eyes shone with laughter when he was amused. She couldn't read his expression now, though.

"You ready to tell me where we're going yet?" she asked as she shouldered her backpack.

"Thought you might enjoy guessing."

She shooed him down the porch steps so she could lock the front door. "You thought wrong. I hate surprises."

She frowned when she spotted his car. Two big white surfboards were sticking out of the back tray.

She shot him a look. "You're aware that Montana is a land-locked state, right?"

"Shows what you know."

She climbed into the truck.

"I think my geography is pretty solid on this one," she said.

"True. But those aren't surfboards."

She twisted to look through the rear window at the boards. Sure enough, now that she saw them up close, they seemed wider than a normal surfboard, and the middle section was covered with what looked like a layer of rubbery matting.

"You've got me," she admitted. "I am officially bamboozled."

"You ever heard of stand-up paddle-boarding?"

"No."

"Then today is going to be a voyage of discovery." He shot her a grin before reversing out into the street.

"And where is this voyage going to take me?"

"Fairy Lake. Any more questions, Your Honor?"

"I'm good for now. But thanks for asking."

His smile was small but it warmed something inside her to know that they understood—and enjoyed—each other so thoroughly.

He headed north, stopping at a truck stop outside of Livingstone for gas. He returned to the car with a couple of coffees and two grease-marked bags. He tossed one into her lap and Tara was about to explain that she wasn't up to eating when the smell of bacon hit her.

Okay, maybe she could make an exception for bacon.

"Oh, this is good," she said as she swallowed her first mouthful of toasted cheese and bacon sandwich.

"Bacon is nature's cure-all," Reid said.

He pulled back onto the freeway, and she took a moment to unwrap his sandwich for him so he wouldn't have to do it one-handed.

"Thanks."

"Least I can do, since you went to all the trouble of getting me out of bed early," she said.

"Just being a good friend."

He was joking, she knew, but it seemed to her that his words were a timely reminder. They'd gone on dozens of cross country runs together, spent time together at the Bozeman firing range, idled away hours manning speed traps talking about their childhoods, past loves, families, but spending time with Reid felt… different now that she no longer had Simon in her life. For the first time since they'd known each other, they were both single, and the knowledge made her feel distinctly edgy.

Get a grip, Buck. This man is your partner, and you are an object of pity right now.

Both excellent points, and she made a promise to herself to keep them front and center in her mind for the rest of the day.

The sandwich and coffee went a long way toward curing her hangover, and by the time Reid had turned off Bridger Canyon Drive and onto Fairy Lake Road she was feeling almost human. Which was just as well, because the final stretch of road was unsealed and creased with runnels and potholes, treating them to a bone-jarring ride for fifteen minutes before they rounded a bend and found themselves looking out over Fairy Lake.

The chalky-white cliffs of Sacagawea Peak towered overhead, its slopes dotted with trees. The lake itself was thickly hemmed by tall pines, the still, deep green waters mirroring the surrounds. It was almost painfully beautiful, and they were both silent as Reid turned off the engine.

"Have you done this before? The paddle-boarding thing?"

"Got my own board and everything." He threw her a small smile before exiting the truck.

She followed him, watching as he hauled first one board then the other from the tray.

"So where did you get the other board, then?" she asked.

"A friend."

"I didn't even know this was a thing," she said, frowning as he collected two long-handled paddles and leaned them against the side of the pickup.

"That's because you've lived a sheltered life."

She knew he was only teasing her, but a part of her bristled. She *had* lived a sheltered life, in many ways. That was what last night—and the motorbike—had been all about.

"Says the professional gypsy. Have you heard about that job in Chicago yet?"

"Yesterday, actually. They want me to come in for a second interview."

"What's wrong? Weren't they bowled over by your many

charms the first time around?"

"Apparently not. Do you need to change? I can take these down to the water to give you privacy."

"I've got my swimsuit on already."

"Then keep your shoes on," Reid advised. "The walk down to the water isn't exactly comfortable barefoot."

He reached for the hem of his T-shirt and pulled it over his head. For a heart-stopping moment she thought he was stripping to bare skin, but he was wearing a form-fitting black tank underneath and she was able to breathe again.

A little alarmed by her reaction, she pulled her own sweater off, leaving her T-shirt on over her bikini top. She could see him taking off his jeans out of the corners of her eyes and she popped the stud on hers, too. She'd done a lot of things with Reid, but none of them had included taking off their clothes together. Even though there was nothing remotely salacious or sexual about the situation, she was still acutely aware of the intimacy of the moment as she turned her back and pushed the denim down her legs.

She folded her jeans and sweater neatly and set them on the passenger seat.

"What can I carry?" she asked as she turned to face him.

She almost stumbled over the last word when she saw that he'd stripped to a pair of dark grey swim shorts that left his long, powerful legs exposed.

That explains the tan, then, a little voice noted in the back of her head.

He lifted one of the boards, his shoulder and arm muscles flexing impressively.

"Bring the paddles, I'll come back for the other board," he said before taking off down the slope toward the lake.

She rolled her eyes. Since when hadn't she pulled her own weight? It took her a moment to locate the handhold molded into the center of the board, then she hefted it and started down the slope after him. He glanced over his shoulder when she was halfway, shaking his head when he saw what she was doing.

"Should have known you wouldn't be able to help yourself," he said.

"Then you shouldn't have bothered telling me not to."

He set his board down near the water's edge and bounded back up the slope at an easy run. She followed him with her eyes until she realized what she was doing, then she snapped her head around and made a big deal out of inspecting the view.

The early morning softness was starting to burn off, and all around her, giant pines reached skyward. She stared at the water, trying to work out what color it was. Emerald green? Azure? A combination of both, perhaps?

She heard the crunch of gravel underfoot as Reid returned.

"It's really beautiful here," she said quietly.

"Yeah. Got to admit, I always feel a little twitchy when I can't see some mountains. One of the side effects of being

Montana born and bred."

She gazed up at Sacagawea Peak. She'd never lived anywhere but Marietta; couldn't imagine not waking up to mountains every day.

"So. How does this behemoth work, anyway?" she asked, turning to contemplate her board.

"It floats. You stand on it, you paddle." He shrugged.

"Right. It's that easy," she said dubiously.

"There are a few little tricks to it. When you start out, stay on your knees and get a feel for the board, what your weight does to it and how the paddle feels in the water. Then, when you're ready, you get to your feet…"

He demonstrated, kneeling on his board and then planting a foot before rising smoothly to his feet.

"You might want to stay squatting and get both feet planted before you attempt to stand. Some people find it easier that way. And once you're up, you want to stay in the center of the board with your feet shoulders-width apart, knees slightly bent. The board's incredibly stable, so as long as you don't flail around you won't fall off."

She glanced out at the water. "I bet it's really cold, huh?"

"Refreshing is the word you're looking for."

"Refreshing. I'll remember that when my extremities start dropping off."

Some of the other lakes in Gallatin County had bathtub-warm water in summer due to their shallowness, but Fairy Lake was not one of them. Tara had swum here a couple of times over the years and knew from experience that it was definitely on the icy side.

"The simple solution is to not fall in," Reid said.

"Right. Thanks for that hot tip."

"When you're paddling, remember you need to work either side to go in a straight line." Again, he demonstrated. "You want to turn, just keep paddling on one side and you'll do a big circle. And for sharper turns, work up a bit of forward momentum, stick your oar straight down and hold on tight, and you should spin around. You need to brace yourself when you do that, though, or you'll fall in."

"Okay. What else?"

"That's about it." He flashed a smile at her. "It's not rocket science."

"I guess not."

He pulled off his sneakers and socks. She followed suit, then copied him again as he carried his board out into the water. He went back for the paddles, passing hers over before pushing his board out until the water was knee-deep.

"Here we go. Paddle placed across the board in front of you. One knee on the board…"

He made it look so easy as he slid first one knee, then the other onto the board and picked up his paddle, looking at her expectantly.

She walked her board out, gasping at how cold the water was. Placing her paddle as he had, she slid her right knee onto the board, then quickly clambered on, her arms stretched out for balance as the board started to rock.

"And you're on. When you start paddling, make sure the blade is fully in the water before pushing so you make the most of your strokes."

"Aye, aye, Captain," she said.

"I was wondering how long it would take for insubordination to rear its ugly head."

"Not long. You should know that by now," she said.

She experimented with a couple of strokes, dipping the oar into the water and propelling the board a few feet across the lake. She was aware of Reid keeping pace with her, watching quietly while she got a sense of the dynamics of it all.

"All good?" he asked.

"I think so."

"Good."

She watched as he rose to his feet with cat-like grace.

"Holler if you need me," he said.

Then he took off, paddle digging deep into the water as he propelled himself forward. He made it look so easy, as though he'd been doing this for a million years.

It was tempting to try standing, but she decided to play it smart and paddle around a little more on her knees first. After ten minutes, she took a deep breath and shifted position so that she was squatting on the board, both feet planted like an ungainly frog. Slowly she rose to her feet. As Reid had promised, the board was very stable and steady.

"Way to go, Starbuck," Reid called across the water.

She shook her head. He knew she hated that nickname. Ever since they'd rebooted the old 80's sci-fi television series Battlestar Gallactica and recast Starbuck as a woman, she'd been taking guff at the station.

She tried a few strokes of the paddle, keeping her knees slightly bent, and slowly her confidence grew. Soon she was able to stop staring at her feet and the paddle and gaze around herself, absorbing the incredible natural beauty surrounding her.

The sun climbed higher in the sky. A gentle breeze caught at her hair and cooled her cheeks. She watched a bird soar high on a thermal, its wings spread wide, and marveled at how it seemed to hang so effortlessly in the sky. When her legs got tired, she got back on her knees, alternating between the two positions as well as sometimes simply sitting with her legs either side of the board, drifting, letting the lake's currents take her where they would.

And slowly, slowly, the peace of the place, the lap of the water, the warmth of the sun began to seep into her bones and the terrible tension she'd been holding within herself all week started to unwind.

Simon, the incident at work, the painful self-realizations she'd had, her uncertainty about what she wanted for the future… she let it all go, let the wind whisk it away, leaving nothing but a quiet, still calm within her.

She was kneeling on her board, sitting back on her heels

as she watched fluffy white clouds scud across the sky when Reid's voice echoed across the water.

"My stomach says it's lunch time. What do you think?"

She started and almost fell off the board. It took her a moment to realize Reid was on the shore, one hand shading his eyes as he watched her.

And he'd taken his tank top off.

Even from a distance, his chest and torso looked amazing. She started paddling back toward shore, feeling absurdly nervous about the prospect of standing on dry land with him with so little clothes on.

Partner. Feels sorry for you. Remember?

Reid waded out into the water to hold the board as she jumped off, dragging it up the bank for her. Her mouth went dry at the way his abdominal muscles rippled with the effort.

God, he had an amazing body. Really, really impressive.

She'd always known that, of course—even the utilitarian cut of the Bozeman PD uniform couldn't disguise his great physique—but seeing him like this, almost naked, was a whole other matter.

His pectoral muscles were cleanly defined, his shoulders broad. His belly was ripped, showcasing his zero percentage body fat. Then there were those thighs, and his beautifully sculpted calves…

She dragged her gaze away from him, concentrating instead on the picnic blanket he'd spread on the wild grass covering the slope, a cooler anchoring one corner.

"It's a long way to the nearest McDonalds," he explained.

"Very efficient of you."

She settled on one side of the blanket while he took the other and started unpacking the cooler. She made a point of concentrating on the food he was unloading instead of him, even though a part of her was desperate to ogle him some more.

In some deep, dark, barely acknowledged corner of her psyche, she'd always wondered what his body was like.

And now she knew.

Food. Concentrate on the food.

There were sandwiches, little baby quiches, some of what looked like his mother's lemon cake, apples—naturally—and two amber-colored glass bottles slick with condensation.

That got her attention, successfully distracting her from his body for a few valuable seconds.

"Please tell me that's Dalton cider?" she asked, already reaching for a bottle.

"Courtesy of Dad. He insisted."

"I freaking love his cider," she said.

Reid's family sold most of their apples to the public or to big retailers, but every year his father set aside a certain quantity for his apple cider run. He only ever pressed a few hundred bottles of the stuff, but it was delicious—sweet and full-flavored and fruity—and she was practically drooling as she remembered the last bottle she'd enjoyed at the department barbecue Reid had hosted at the Dalton's place earlier in the year.

"Better enjoy it, then."

There was a dark note to his voice and she risked a look at him. He was gazing out at the lake, a grim set to his mouth.

"Why do you say that?"

He shrugged, and she got the sense that he wished he could take back his words. "It's a limited resource. You know that. Have a sandwich."

He unwrapped his own, taking a big bite.

She mustered all her resolve and managed to stop her gaze from drifting below his chin as she continued to study him.

"Is something going on with the orchard? Is your dad okay?"

Reid frowned, then glanced down at his sandwich. Really wishing he hadn't said anything now if she had a guess.

"You started it, Dalton," she pointed out.

"Thanks for reminding me."

She took a swig from her cider and unwrapped her sandwich. Chicken, mayo and walnuts. Yum.

"You might as well tell me. I'll get it out of you eventually."

"Going to use your stellar interrogation technique on me, are you?"

"You want to tell me. You wouldn't have said anything otherwise. Might as well just cut to the chase."

He took a long pull from his cider, then tilted the bottle and studied the amber glass for a long beat. She pretended that she didn't want to reach out and wrap her hand around his gorgeously developed biceps and munched away on her sandwich.

"Mom wants to sell the place."

Tara frowned, jerked out of her preoccupation by his words. The Daltons had grown apples for three generations. Selling up would mean giving all that away. Abandoning a legacy.

"Only your mom?"

"She hasn't brought it up with Dad yet. But Mom's pretty persuasive when she's on the warpath. And there's no doubting that the accident shook him up a lot. Who knows? Maybe he'll be relieved to be able to walk away."

"I take it this has come up because you don't want it?"

He frowned, almost as though her words had irritated him. "Something like that."

"Well, either you do, or you don't. I assume your folks wouldn't sell if you were going to step in at some point."

"Maybe we should drop this." He crumpled up the plastic wrap from his sandwich.

Wow, she'd really touched a nerve.

"Do you want the orchard or not, Reid?"

"It's not as black and white as that."

"Why not?"

He sighed, his mouth curling up at the corners as he threw her a rueful look. "You're like a dog with a bone sometimes, you know that?"

She growled deep in her throat before giving him her best dog bark.

"That is… wrong on so many levels," he said.

But he was smiling now.

"Tell me why it isn't as simple as black and white." Having polished off her sandwich, she reached for a baby quiche.

"Because it's not just about me. My grandfather bought that land and cleared it. Planted more than three hundred trees by hand. It doesn't feel like it's mine to give up."

"But you don't want to be tied down by it?"

He ran a hand through his hair. "I used to hate the place, when I was younger. Resented the hell out of it. Took off the moment I could."

"Funny, I thought you'd enjoyed helping your dad out this past year. At least, that was the sense I got." He'd never complained about having to spend his downtime in the orchard. Not once.

"I don't mind the work. Not anymore. In a lot of ways, it's really rewarding."

"But you don't want to be tied down?"

He finished his bottle of cider before responding, setting the bottle carefully back in the basket. His father recycled them, she knew.

"I guess I just never imagined my whole life being played out in Marietta."

"Then I guess that's your answer, then."

She felt sad as she said it. She liked having Reid around. Working with him and getting to know him had been a privilege.

Looking at him wasn't too bad, either.

She distracted herself from her inappropriate and dangerous thoughts by helping herself to a piece of lemon cake. Once she'd demolished that, she brushed the crumbs off her T-shirt and lay back with her ankles crossed, arms behind her head, and closed her eyes.

If her eyes were closed, she wouldn't be tempted to keep staring at him. That was the theory, anyway.

In practice, she was almost preternaturally aware of him moving around, putting food back in the cooler, rearranging things.

"Here," he said, and she opened her eyes to find him leaning over her.

He was so close she could see the individual hairs of his eyelashes and she drew in a nervous breath. Then she realized he'd folded her towel into a pillow for her and was waiting for her to lift her head so he could position it for her.

"Thanks."

She engaged her belly muscles and lifted her head and shoulders, and he slid the folded towel into place. She was powerless to stop herself from breathing in the smell of him as he did so—deodorant and sun-warmed skin and man.

He was back on his side of the blanket in no seconds flat, arranging his own towel in a similar fashion. Her gaze got caught on the dark silk of the hair beneath his arms before darting to the sexy little trail that led beneath the waistband of his shorts. Parts of him she didn't normally see. Parts of him she'd always wondered about.

Traitorous heat unfolded in the pit of her stomach. When she and Scarlett were teenagers, her sister's bedroom walls had been covered with posters of hot guys in various states of undress, but Tara's bedroom walls had been all about the athletes she admired and the movies she loved. She'd never considered herself the type of woman who ogled men or got all squirmy when a well-built guy happened into her orbit.

What a fool.

She concentrated on her breathing, aware that her heart was beating too fast. She needed to calm the hell down and stop thinking like this. If Reid knew what was going on in her head… she didn't even want to contemplate how embarrassing that would be.

Instead, she thought about work, and her mom, and how happy she was that Scarlett had found Mitch—although, strictly speaking, it had been the other way around, since Mitch had come looking for Scarlett, tracking her all the way from the Australian outback to Marietta.

Gradually her hyper-awareness faded and she breathed a

sigh of relief.

"So, you ever going to get around to telling me about this motorbike?"

Chapter Eight

REID'S VOICE WAS lazy and relaxed, but it didn't stop her eyes from popping open.

"I thought we covered that last night."

"I can think of a million better ways to live a little than buying a motorbike," he said.

She turned her head to find him watching her. If it was anyone else, she'd tell them where to stuff it, but she could see the concern in his espresso-dark eyes.

"Maybe you can. But this is about what I want, and I want that bike."

"You said something last night. About being sick of waiting for people to leave you."

Three cheers for her beer-lubricated mouth.

"Did I?"

"Tell me you don't think you had anything to do with Simon cheating on you? Because that is straight-up bullshit, Tara. It's all on him, all of it."

He sat up, no longer lazy and relaxed. Not wanting to be at a disadvantage, she sat up, too.

"I don't think it's my fault he cheated. But it's my fault for being with him. That's all on me."

He frowned and she could see he didn't understand.

"It's hard to explain," she said, thinking about all the elements that had fed into the unconscious decision she'd made to play it safe with Simon. Her father, her mother, the way things had been after he left...

And then suddenly she was talking, the words pouring out of her, almost as though she'd been waiting for an opportunity to share this part of herself with him.

"When my dad left, my mom fell apart. She loved him so much, and she just... couldn't cope without him, I guess. She was so wounded and hurt and broken, and for a long time all she did was cry and spend days in bed and talk on the phone with Aunt Margot." Tara swallowed past the tightness in her throat. She couldn't think about those hard times without getting emotional. Life had been so precarious, every day had felt as though it balanced on the edge of disaster. "I felt so guilty. So responsible. I did everything I could to help out, but I couldn't bring Dad back and that was what she wanted, more than anything."

"Your dad didn't leave because of you and Scarlett, Tara," Reid said.

"I know. But something happened before he left..." She drew her knees to her chest and looped her arms around them, needing the comfort as she gathered her courage. Then, her gaze fixed on the red and black plaid of the picnic blanket, she told him what she'd never told anyone else. "I came home from school early one day. I had a dentist appointment, and I was supposed to meet Mom at home and she was going to drive me to Dr. Cassidy's. She wasn't home when I got there, though. Dad was. And he was with someone. I could hear them when I let myself in, and I found them in the kitchen, kissing, half-undressed."

She had to stop then, the old memory so powerful she felt physically ill. Reid shifted, turning to face her, reaching out to wrap his hand around her ankle. His touch was so reassuring, so grounding and safe, and she lifted her gaze from the blanket briefly to look at him.

His expression was patiently solemn as he waited for more.

"He told me it was a mistake," she said. "Told me it would never happen again. He cried… I'd never seen him like that. He made me promise that I would never tell anyone. He said he'd make it up to Mom, to me, to all of us. And I believed him."

She saw comprehension dawn in Reid's eyes.

"How long was it until he left?" he asked, his voice gravelly with what she suspected was anger.

And why not? It was an angry-making story. Her father had behaved appallingly. Weakly. Shamefully.

"A month. Just long enough for him to arrange things to suit himself. Take money from the mortgage, sort out a new place to live. Then we came home from school one day and he was gone and Mom was… broken."

And Tammy Buck had never recovered, and Tara has spent the last thirteen years wondering what might have happened if she'd said something about what she'd seen, instead of honoring her promise to her father.

"Your father is an asshole."

Trust Reid to put it so bluntly.

"Yeah, he is. But we all loved him like crazy when he was around. Then he just faded out of our lives, skipping visitation weekends, putting us off until it became clear that he'd rather forget he had us than face up to his own guilt. We haven't heard from him in ten years."

His hand tightened around her ankle. She took a deep breath, determined to get it all out.

"Anyway. Like I said, I did my best to make it up to Mom for not telling her about that day. To make things okay. But I always felt as though there was something I should have done. Warned Mom. Something. That's why I always drop everything when she needs me. Why I can't say no to her or Scarlett."

"Jesus, Tara. It wasn't your fault. You must know that."

"I do. It took a while, but I worked out that I was carrying around my dad's guilt for him, and that it wasn't my burden to bear. I actually thought I was on top of it, which is pretty hilarious in retrospect. It took everything blowing up with Simon for me to realize that I'd been working so hard trying to avoid my mother's fate that I'd almost married a man I didn't love."

Reid's hand tightened around her ankle again, and she forced herself to look up and meet his eyes.

He looked… shaken. And also a little confused. She smiled ruefully. Apparently she'd done such a great job of convincing herself she loved Simon that she'd convinced the world, too.

"You look like Scarlett did when I told her. She actually argued with me. Tried to convince me I was wrong, that I was mad about him," she said.

"I thought you were. When he asked you to marry him… you were happy."

His gaze searched her face as he tried to understand.

"I was happy. He was safe, right? He wasn't going anywhere. He wasn't some outgoing, foot-loose, fancy-free raconteur like my father. He was a history teacher."

She almost laughed at her own naivety and stupidity.

"So you're not…?"

"Heartbroken? No. I'm hurt. He betrayed my trust. I feel stupid, humiliated. But my heart is fine."

There was a profound silence as they looked at one another.

"That's good. I mean, the rest of it isn't, but that part is good." His hand slipped free from her ankle, releasing her.

"Yeah. And that stuff at work last week? My Incredible Hulk impersonation? That was me starting to realize how badly I'd almost messed up my life."

Reid nodded, processing. "I can see that."

"I made myself a promise when I worked all this out the other night. No more playing it safe."

"Right. Which brings us back to the motorbike."

"Yep."

He looked out at the lake, clearly chewing something over. "Promise me you'll be careful on the damned thing, okay?"

"Yes, Mr. Dalton."

He shook his head at her.

"Such a smart ass," he said.

"Thanks. I've been taking lessons from this guy I know."

"Sweetheart, that attitude is all yours, and you know it."

They were both smiling, and something shifted between them. Suddenly she was very aware of how little they were both wearing, and the fact that they were utterly alone. Reid's smile faded and he looked out at the lake again, a frown on his face.

"I might see if I can catch up on a little sleep," she said, settling back onto the blanket. "All that cider and food has made me sleepy."

"Good idea."

She settled back onto her towel pillow, and this time she fell into a true drowse, warmed by the sun and Reid's concern.

He cared about her. He might be leaving soon, but he cared about her.

She had no idea how long she dozed, but gradually she came back to consciousness. When she opened her eyes, Reid was standing beside the blanket, stretching his arms high over his head, his skin burnished by the sun. She blinked as she gazed up at six-foot-two of rock-solid muscle.

It was almost enough to make you believe in the gods of Olympus, it really was.

"You up for another go?" Reid asked when he realized she was awake.

"Sure am."

She stood, and together they walked down to the water's edge. She felt like an old pro as she pushed her board out to knee-deep water. Reid followed suit, and they both paddled out into deeper water before standing.

"Come check out the other side of the lake," Reid said, pointing with his paddle.

His strokes were longer and more powerful than hers, but she did her best to keep up, carefully rationing the number of times she allowed herself to admire his back and butt along the way.

She was only flesh and blood, after all.

When they got to the other side, he pointed out some wildflowers that had sprouted in a fallen log, and they drifted along the edge of the lake, talking and laughing. The sun moved across the sky as they did a slow tour, waving to two hikers and their dog on the far side of the lake, stopping to watch a deer that was grazing in the dappled light beneath the trees.

She was the one who suggested a race, taking shameless advantage by taking off at a fast clip before Reid could turn his board around. It didn't take long for him to start gaining on her and Tara pushed her oar deep with each stroke, willing her board across the water. She wasn't sure what happened—whether she hit something and the board jostled, or if she'd simply rocked herself off balance putting so much effort into her paddling, but one second she was laughing gleefully over the fact that she was somehow maintaining her lead, and the next the board seemed to slide sideways out from beneath her feet and she was teetering over the water.

She let out a cry of despair.

And then she was in the water, and it was every bit as icy as she knew it would be as she flailed her way to the surface.

The first thing she heard when she came up for air was the sound of Reid's laughter, deep and masculine, echoing off the water.

Kicking her feet, she stretched out a hand for her board before using her free hand to push the hair out of her eyes.

"Nice. Thanks for the empathy, Sir Galahad," she said.

"How's the water?"

"Delightful."

He laughed again. She gave him a disgruntled look before dragging herself across the board and shuffling around until she was lying lengthwise on the damned thing, fully aware that she probably looked about as gracious and graceful as a beached sea cow while doing all of the above.

Finally she was on her feet again, flipping her dripping hair over her shoulder. Her T-shirt clung to her like glue, and she took a moment to make sure her bathing suit was covering everything it should be.

"So, want to make it the best out of three?" Reid asked, his expression deceptively innocent.

"Absolutely."

"And maybe we could both start at the same time this time?" he suggested, eyebrows raised.

"Sorry?" she said.

His smile was knowing as he paddled his board alongside hers.

"On three," he said. "First to the big boulder. One, two, three."

She waited until he had his blade deep in the water midway through his first stroke before reaching across with her paddle and prodding him firmly in the ass. His head snapped around, an expression of comic outrage on his face, but it was too late, he was already off balance.

She grinned as he hit the water with an almighty splash. Her amusement faded when Reid didn't surface immediately, and she leaned forward to peer into the water. His board was in the way, however, and the water was too murky at this depth.

"Reid?" she called out, panic hitting her. What if he'd hit his head on his board on the way down and she hadn't noticed, or there was a submerged log he'd gotten caught on…?

She was about to throw her paddle aside and dive in when her board tilted ever-so-slightly to the rear. She glanced over her shoulder to see Reid gripping the tail, a fiendishly evil grin on his face.

"No."

"I'm afraid so, cupcake."

He pushed down, the board went up, and she went in, arms flailing. He was laughing once again when she resurfaced.

"Okay. I may have deserved that," she conceded.

"You think?"

This time around she didn't have the benefit of sun-warmed skin to keep her warm and she could feel the chill seeping into her limbs.

"Maybe we should call a truce before we both turn into icicles," she said.

"Sounds like a plan." He swam toward her, offering her his hand.

She eyed it mistrustfully.

"What's wrong? You think I'm going to dunk you?" he asked, looking as mischievous as a little boy.

"I know you are, so don't play all innocent with me."

He took her hand anyway, but the smile quickly left his mouth as he grasped it.

"You're freezing."

"Amazing powers of perception you have there."

"Get back on your board," he ordered, his eyebrows knitting into a frown.

"What a good idea. Why didn't I think of that?"

She reached for her board, once again bellying her way onto it and shuffling around until she was lengthwise rather than across it. Reid, she noted sourly, managed to somehow almost vault out of the water onto his, the big showoff.

She stayed on her knees when she was done, shivering as the wind hit her already cold skin.

"Let's head for shore," Reid said. "We should probably think about going home, anyway."

He wasn't going to get any argument from her. Suddenly the jeans and sweater she'd left in the truck seemed like her idea of heaven.

She stayed on her knees as she paddled back to shore, slipping off in the shallows and dragging the board up onto the bank. Her towel was warm from the sun when she wrapped it around her shoulders and buried her face in it, inhaling the smell of warm terrycloth and detergent.

"Oh, that is so nice."

"You should take that wet T-shirt off," Reid said.

She lifted her face from the warmth of the towel to find him standing there dripping all over the blanket.

"Probably a good idea," she conceded.

She let her towel drop, reaching for the hem of her T-shirt and dragging it up her body. It wasn't until she let it slip to the ground that she glanced down and realized her nipples were hard from the cold, creating two very noticeable points in her aqua blue bikini top. She bent down to collect the towel, carefully tucking it around her torso and securing the end beneath her armpit before looking at Reid.

He was busy toweling himself off, and she told herself he probably hadn't even noticed. Anyway, she was cold. Nipples did the sticking-out thing when people were cold. His were a little puckered, too, she noticed.

Then he glanced across and caught her checking out his nipples and heat rocketed up her chest and into her face.

"I should take the cooler up to the car," she said, turning away to go fetch her sneakers.

She made sure her feet were thoroughly dry before pulling on her socks and shoes, the small task giving her ample opportunity to avoid looking at Reid. Then she grabbed the cooler and lugged it up the slope. Reid passed her on the way back down, one of the boards under his arm.

"Leave the other board for me," he ordered before continuing up the bank.

She considered disobeying him, but she was fully aware that going up the slope was going to be a lot harder than coming down, and the board was big and cumbersome. Instead, she folded the picnic blanket and collected her wet T-shirt and Reid's tank top and headed for the car.

"Good girl," Reid said when he saw she'd listened to him.

"Don't push your luck."

He was smiling as he walked down the hill.

She collected her clothes from the front seat, then glanced around, trying to work out where she could change. There were plenty of pine trees, but not much underbrush, and none of the tree trunks were wide enough to act as a makeshift screen.

Reid appeared, slinging the board into the bed of the truck.

"You take one side, I take the other, and we both pretend we're gentlemen," he said, somehow reading her mind.

"That's going to be a stretch for one of us," she said.

He laughed. "I surely do hope so."

She realized what she'd said then, and couldn't help laughing, too. He moved to the other side of the truck, and she turned her back and pulled her underwear from the backpack. She tried to keep the towel tucked beneath her armpits as she shimmied out of her wet swimsuit, but it kept slipping and in the end she let it drop in the interests of simply getting her underwear on sooner rather than later. The warm cotton felt better than silk against her skin, and soon she was pulling on her jeans and sweater.

"That feels better," she said.

"Does that mean you're decent?"

"No, I'm standing here in my birthday suit, dancing a jig."

"I've never seen you dance."

Reid walked around the front of the truck, his eyes alight with amusement. She couldn't stop her gaze from dropping to his chest. Now that she knew what was beneath his clothes, she would probably never be truly comfortable in his presence again.

A rather alarming thought, given they worked with each other.

Not for long, remember? He's heading to Chicago soon.

He was. And if it wasn't Chicago, it would be somewhere else. So maybe it was okay for her to let herself admire him in his hip- and thigh-hugging jeans that were faded in all the right places.

"Your nose is a little pink," he said.

"That'll happen."

He grabbed her backpack and stowed it in the back of the truck while she liberated a couple of apples from the cooler, tossing one to him when he'd finished. They were both biting into crisp sweetness as he began the bone-jangling trip back to the freeway.

"Can I ask you something?" he said.

"You can."

"That stuff about your dad… have you ever talked to your mom or sister about that?"

"No. And I don't plan to." She frowned at him, not sure what he was thinking. Her mom would hate her if she found out what had happened that afternoon. Tara knew it with every bone in her body. Tammy Buck would work on that single piece of information in her mind until she'd turned it into a missed opportunity, and Tara didn't want to upset her when her mother was already grappling to come to terms with her Parkinson's disease.

"Your decision. It just occurred to me that it might be good to talk it over with your sister. Scare a few ghosts out of the closet."

"That ghost is an old one. I'm happy to leave it where it is, thanks."

"Like I said, your call."

She made an effort to shift the conversation then, asking him about his second job interview in Chicago and ragging on him about wearing a suit.

"I can't imagine you all gussied up," she said.

"Like a bear in a tuxedo, you think?"

"Yeah. Exactly like that."

"I have it on good authority that I scrub up okay."

"Pretty sure your mom doesn't count, Reid."

That earned her a smile.

"I have other people willing to vouch for me."

"I bet."

They stopped for dinner in Livingstone on the way through, both of them having worked up an appetite, and they rolled into Marietta just as dusk began to blur the world and the street lights were flickering on.

Tara felt an odd sense of disappointment as Reid turned into her driveway and cruised toward her townhouse. It had been such a great day, she'd felt so good, enjoyed Reid so much…

She didn't want it to end.

The knowledge burned in her belly as he came to a halt in front of her single-car garage, slipping the car into neutral.

"Fair warning, you might have sore legs and feet tomorrow from all the work counterbalancing on the board," he said.

"Noted. I'll be sure to remember you fondly as I hobble around."

"You do that."

She twisted to face him, her gaze going over his mussed hair and his beard-shadowed cheeks. He'd given her a much-needed circuit break today, taking her away from all the crap she'd been marinating in and blowing fresh air into her head. He'd also listened and let her vent without judging or trying to solve anything.

"Thank you," she said. "I think you might have just saved my ass today."

"Only your ass? I'll have to lift my game." His smile was small and slightly self-conscious.

Typical Reid, bold in everything except accepting heartfelt appreciation.

"You've been a good friend to me, Reid Dalton. I'm going to miss you like hell when you abandon us and head to Chicago."

"Might not get the job yet. Don't go counting your

chickens."

"They'd be crazy not to take you."

She scooted across her seat a little and leaned in to kiss his cheek. They didn't normally kiss and hug or do any of that touch-feely stuff, but it felt right for today. It felt necessary.

Her hand landed on his shoulder, and she inhaled the good, fresh scent of him as she pressed her lips to his cheek. She must have surprised him, because he shifted a little and his stubble rasped across her lips, the lightest of abrasions.

She pulled away, instinctively licking her lips to soothe them. Reid's gaze followed the movement, and she was close enough to see his pupils dilate and his nostrils flare.

She went very still. And then she did something she'd been wanting to do for a very long time: she leaned close and kissed him, properly this time.

His mouth was warm, and she could taste the sweetness of the lemon meringue pie he'd had for dessert. She waited for him to respond, to do something, but he seemed to be waiting for something else. Something more.

Well, might as well go for it. Feeling bolder than bold, she ran her tongue along the closed seam of his lips, asking for entry. There was the smallest of pauses, then some of the tension went out of him as he opened to her, his tongue stroking hers, his mouth starting to move at last. His hands found her waist, his fingers gripping her warmly as his kiss became more demanding, more urgent.

God, yes. Urgent was how she felt, and she'd never been greedier, more ready, more eager in her life. Her heart was already racing, her body flooding with heat, the need for more, more, more a drumbeat in the back of her head.

She made a small encouraging sound as his hand left her hip and smoothed its way up her torso. If he touched her breasts, she was pretty sure she could almost come on the spot.

Suddenly he stilled, pulling back slightly so he could look her in the eye.

"Tara... this is a bad idea."

"No, it isn't." It was the best idea she'd had in a long time. "You'll be going soon. I know that. But I want to know before you go, Reid. I need to know."

A whole year they'd been sitting side by side in that damned patrol car, denying the pull of desire between them.

She was sick of denying it. She was sick of playing it safe.

His gaze searched her face, and whatever it was he saw seemed to satisfy him, because the next thing she knew he was kissing her as though his life depended on it.

Fierce and demanding, taking no prisoners. She gripped his shoulders as his hand slid onto her breast, the friction of his thumb gliding over her nipple making her shudder with need.

It felt so good, he tasted so good. Operating on blind instinct, she threw a leg over the center console and slid into his lap.

"Jesus, Tara," he said, his hands gripping her ass as she straddled him.

They kissed again, bodies grinding together. He pushed a hand beneath her sweater, tugging her bra out of the way to reach her breast.

She couldn't get enough. The taste of him. The feel of his hands on her body. She was on fire, her sex hot and wet for him. All she could think about was having him inside her, filling her. She slid a hand between their bodies, feeling the hard, long length of him through his jeans.

This. She wanted this. She wanted it now.

She fumbled at the stud on her jeans, breaking their kiss so she could maneuver more easily.

"What are you doing?" Reid asked, his eyes glinting in the darkness.

"What does it look like I'm doing?"

She rolled to the side, already pushing her jeans down her legs, taking her panties with them.

"Don't worry, I'm on the pill," she said.

Reid's hand found her bare ass as she kicked off her jeans, his fingers curling into her flesh possessively.

"Just as long as you know we're in the driveway in front of your townhouse," he said, and she could hear both the amusement and the desire in his voice.

"I can't wait."

She couldn't, and it was dark enough and they were private enough down here at the end, away from her neighbors.

Reid took care of his belt buckle and button fly, and together they pulled his jeans down. His erection sprang free, thick and long and hard, and she wrapped her hand around it, reveling in how hot he was.

Need driving her, she straddled him once again and guided him into place. The exquisite pressure of him filling her, stretching her, made her clutch at his shoulders as she took him all. His hand slid to the back of her neck, squeezing lightly.

"Give me a second," he said, his voice very low, his hand holding her still.

She understood. She'd expected it to be good, but she hadn't expected it to be profound.

This felt right. Right and so good and absolutely essential.

Reid pressed his mouth to her neck. "I've wanted this for a long time."

"Me, too."

Even though she'd been too scared, too stupid, too blind to acknowledge it.

His hands found her hips as he thrust up into her, and together they started to move, quickly finding a rhythm that was all their own. Reid's hands slid from her hips and up her torso, pushing her sweater out of the way. She leaned forward, offering him her breasts and he took her left nipple into his mouth and tongued it avidly.

She was so wet, so aroused, she could already feel her

climax bearing down on her. She drove her fingers into his hair, holding him to her as she rode him. He switched to her other breast, biting her nipple gently before drawing it into his mouth.

"Reid," she breathed.

And then she came apart, sensation rippling through her in delicious waves, her sex throbbing around him, her knees locked to his sides.

One of his hands found her ass, pulling her more tightly to him, and he thrust himself deep, his whole body shuddering as he found his own pleasure.

She was breathing hard, her body damp with sweat, her breasts and face tender from his stubble. And yet she'd never felt better, more alive, more herself than ever before in her life.

Bowing her head, she rested it on Reid's shoulder, pressing a kiss to his skin.

She would never regret this. Ever.

Chapter Nine

Reid woke to the smell of apple blossom. Stirring lazily, he smiled as memories from last night rushed over him. Then he pushed Tara's hair out of his face, sliding a hand around her body and tucking himself more snuggly behind her.

They'd slept well together, he and Tara—when they'd finally slept. She'd asked if they could go back to his place rather than do the obvious and go to hers. He had been more than happy to eschew the ghosts of her former relationship, driving out to the orchard and kissing her every step of the way up the stairs to his apartment.

They'd barely made it to the bed the second time, tearing each other's clothes off, the room echoing with their roughly-voiced words of encouragement and appreciation. Making love to Tara had been… extraordinary, in the truest sense of the word.

He'd never had such intense, fun, gratifying sex in his life, and just lying here thinking about it was making him hard all over again.

He nudged his hips a little closer, enjoying the pressure of her ass against his erection. She stirred, her behind pressing back into him more firmly, and he realized she was awake.

"Morning," he murmured, pressing a kiss to her shoulder.

"Morning."

She was smiling. He couldn't see her face, but he knew it. Could feel it.

He spread his hand over her belly. Her skin was soft and warm, and she smelled so good, like sunshine and soap.

"I have a question for you," he said.

"Mmmm?" She wiggled her backside against him, teasing him shamelessly.

"Are you a morning person?" he asked, gliding his hand down her belly and into the silk of her pubic hair. She was wet and swollen with wanting and he got even harder as he stroked the seam of her sex.

"What do you think?" she asked.

He shifted, rolling on top of her, and she welcomed him with widespread thighs and arms. This would be their fourth time making love, and he still had to stop himself from simply plunging inside her, his need for her was so powerful.

Instead, he kept a tight rein on himself, using his erection to tease her, sliding back and forth, loving the way her head dropped back and her mouth opened, her teeth just showing as she started to pant.

"Want me?" he asked.

"Yes. Stop being a tease."

Her hands gripped his ass, encouraging him to push inside her, and he gave into her urging, beginning the slow slide to ecstasy. She lifted her legs, locking them behind his hips, and he slid his hands under her ass and used his grip to tilt her hips as he stroked into her.

She was flushed and tousle-haired, her green eyes cloudy with desire, her nipples budded into taut peaks. He drew one into his mouth, savoring the taste of her, relishing all the little sounds she made: the catch of her breath, the low moan in the back of her throat when he stroked her deeply, the little rushed exhale as he stepped up the pace.

He stoked her desire, holding his own in check, until finally he couldn't wait a second longer. She panted out her encouragement as he pounded into her, then he felt her tighten around him, and she was gone, her gaze dazed and shaken and lost as she came.

Her pleasure fed his, and he pressed his face into her neck and inhaled the essence of her as he gave himself up, his body shuddering into hers.

Her arms held him tightly afterward, denying him when he would have rolled away to relieve her of his weight. He was only too happy to stay. In fact, if he had his way, the world would stop turning altogether so they could remain like this forever.

"What's your best guess?" she asked, her voice husky and

low.

"About what?"

"Whether I'm a morning person or not?"

He was still inside her, and he felt her muscles tighten around him. He smiled against her neck.

"I'm thinking yes."

"I'm thinking I might be an afternoon and evening person, too, when it comes to you."

He lifted his head so he could see her face, supporting himself on his elbows. She had a strand of hair across her forehead and he brushed it gently away. She watched him a little warily, although her lips were smiling.

"Tara—"

"No, don't. Let's not say all the things that need to be said. Let's just enjoy this while it lasts. Be a little reckless."

He brushed a thumb along her cheekbone. She was so freaking gorgeous. It made his chest tight, being this close to her and seeing the many different shades of green in her eyes.

"Okay. If that's the way you want it."

"It is."

"There's still the small matter of work."

"But not for much longer."

"As much as I enjoy your faith in me, I haven't got the job yet."

"You will."

Her confidence in him was simple and unequivocal, and he brushed his thumb along her cheekbone again.

"We'll see."

A knock echoed through the apartment, and they both glanced over his shoulder toward the door.

"That's locked, right?" Tara asked a little nervously.

"It should be."

"Reid?" His mother's voice sounded clearly through the door. "I'm making waffles. Should I save some for you?"

"Yes, please," he called.

Tara started to giggle quietly.

"Tara would like some, too," he added.

Her eyes went wide then, and she slapped his shoulder, doing her best to push him off her.

There was a telling silence. Then:

"I'll open up another bottle of syrup. Morning, Tara."

"Morning, Mrs. Dalton."

"Judy is fine, dear."

They heard the sound of his mother retreating down the staircase and Tara gave a mighty heave, successfully wriggling out from under him.

"That was a dirty stunt, Dalton."

"I thought you liked waffles?"

"You are lucky you are so good in bed. That's all I'll say for now."

She slid to the edge of the bed, evading him again as she stood and headed for the bathroom.

"I need a shower."

The thought of Tara naked beneath streaming water was

enough to have him bounding out of bed to go after her. Her smile was small but knowing as he joined her beneath the spray.

"What took you so long?"

They ran the tank dry washing each other, and when they emerged the bathroom was cloaked in steamy fog. He flicked on the exhaust fan and dried himself off, watching while Tara did the same. She was so freaking sexy, with her long, athletic legs and slim hips. As for her breasts… he'd lost sleep fantasizing about her breasts, and they more than lived up to his imagination, her nipples a pale browny-pink, the shape round and full.

"I thought you wanted waffles?" she said, giving his crotch a significant look.

He was hard again, his erection straining against his belly.

"You're the one standing there all naked and gorgeous," he said, hooking an arm around her waist and kissing her.

She let him have his way for a few minutes before pulling back.

"I don't suppose your parents will believe I slept on the couch."

He smiled slowly. "Why, Ms. Buck, don't tell me you're shy?"

"No." She frowned slightly. "It's just they know about Simon and that we work together and it might be weird."

"My mother is probably in the kitchen doing a victory

dance," he said. "She loves you. They both do."

She looked pensive for a second, then she shrugged. "All right. I'm sure I'll survive the walk of shame." She turned to head into the bedroom.

He frowned, reaching for her and pulling her back into his arms. "There wasn't an ounce of shame in what we did last night."

She looked a little surprised by his vehemence. "I know. Sorry, that was a bad choice of words."

He studied her face, needing to be sure that she meant what she said.

"It's okay, Reid. I want to be here. I don't regret anything. I couldn't." She pressed a kiss to his mouth before exiting to the bedroom.

They dressed in silence, then Tara brushed her wet hair and pulled it into a ponytail and announced herself ready to face the music and the waffles.

He led the way downstairs and across to the main house, slipping his hand into hers as they entered the foyer.

"In the kitchen," his father called as the door clicked shut behind them.

Tara stood a little taller, and he kissed her quickly. "Don't be an idiot."

"Good morning," his mother said brightly as they arrived in the kitchen.

Four places were set around the old oak table, and a pitcher of freshly squeezed orange juice sat in the middle, along with a jug of maple syrup.

"Hope you're hungry," his mother said, her gaze bouncing from him to Tara and back again.

"Come sit next to me, Tara," his father said, pushing the seat out for her with his foot.

Tara smiled at them both. "Thanks. And I am hungry, thank you."

His father started talking about the weather, and his mother dished up the first round of waffles. Sitting across the table from Tara, he watched as she slowly relaxed.

As he'd said, his parents loved her. Far from disapproving of the idea of the two of them together, they were far more likely to push him to make it permanent, his parents never having been shy about their desire to see him happily settled.

A concept that had always sent shivers up his spine—until recently.

The whole notion of being "settled" had always conjured up visions of making-do and conceding in his mind. But that wasn't how he felt when he looked across the table at Tara. She wasn't a concession, she was the grand prize. She was a lifetime of laughter and generosity and challenge.

When he looked at her, he didn't feel trapped. He didn't want to check the specials board at the local travel agents. He didn't want to loosen his collar and check where the exits were.

She made him want to stop and stay.

"Reid? Are you with us or not?"

He glanced up to find his mother standing beside him, a plate full of waffles in hand.

"Sorry, did you say something?"

"I asked how many do you want?"

"As many as you're prepared to give me."

His mother was frowning slightly as she loaded up his plate and he wondered how long she'd been standing there.

The waffles were great, and Tara's bright smile and sparky comebacks to his dad reassured him that she'd let go of any misgivings she had about going public with his parents regarding their... situation.

Because it was too early to call it a relationship, even though everything in him wanted to. There were too many question marks hanging over everything for him to let himself go there. Tara might be whole-hearted after her break up, but there was no getting away from the fact that she was still recovering from the wreckage of her engagement. And then there was the Chicago job to consider.

Tara insisted on helping clean up after breakfast before suggesting it was time she went home. She still had to collect her pickup from The Wolves Den across town, and she had "things to do."

"We can head into town now," he said as they both hung up their kitchen towels to dry.

"Thanks. And thanks, Judy, for a great breakfast. Best waffles I've had for a long time."

"Vanilla essence in the batter," his mom said with a

wink. "Works every time."

Reid stared at her. His mother was notoriously cagey about her recipes, yet here she was, handing out one of her most closely guarded secrets without being held at gunpoint.

"I'll have to remember that," Tara said.

"Reid, I need help in the laundry room, if I can borrow you for a moment," his mother said. "It will only take a second."

The look she gave him was loaded with meaning.

"I'll wait outside," Tara said diplomatically.

His mother disappeared into the laundry room and Reid took a deep breath and followed her. The moment they were alone, his mother pushed the door closed.

"What are you doing, Reid Dalton?" she hissed the moment it thudded shut. "That poor girl has just had her whole life turned upside down, and all you can think to do is snake-charm her into your bed?"

He flinched away from the vehemence of her words, a little taken aback by the depth of her feeling.

"Whoa. You want to calm down there a minute?"

"I know you've always had a thing for her, but she is not one of your easy-come, easy-go women, Reid. I'm really disappointed that you've allowed your libido to put you in a situation where you're going to hurt a person who deserves a lot better."

He was starting to get irritated by all the assumptions his mom was making. Sure, he hadn't dated anyone steadily since he came home to Montana, but he wasn't an alley cat.

"I didn't realize you had such a high opinion of my morals," he said sharply.

His mother set her hands on her hips and eyed him critically.

"I love you, but I'm not so one-eyed I can't see your faults. You're charming and handsome, and women have always come too easily to you. Which is fine, except when they want things that you aren't prepared to give."

"You have no idea what I'm prepared to give Tara," he said.

"A home? Your heart? A ring? Because those are the things that Tara wants and needs."

"You know what? I'm not having this conversation with you. What's going on between Tara and me is our business, and I don't have to justify myself or explain myself to you."

"No, you do not. But I just hope you can look yourself in the eye when you go sailing off to this new job in Chicago and leave her behind."

"For Pete's sake, will everyone stop going on about the Chicago job as though I've got it already? It's a second interview. Nothing is set in stone."

"If it's not this job, it will be another one, Reid. Be honest with yourself, at least. You always leave. The grass is always greener, life is always elsewhere. And that's okay, it really is, as long as you don't set up expectations that you aren't going to fulfill."

"You must think I'm a real asshole," he said, thoroughly pissed off now.

He yanked the door open and exited angrily to the kitchen before heading for the front door. Tara was waiting by his truck, her head downturned, when he emerged from the house.

She scanned his face as he approached. "You okay?"

"Yep."

He held her door open for her, and she considered him for a beat before climbing into the truck.

She waited until they were pulling out of the driveway and onto the road into town before speaking.

"I hope you and your mom didn't fight over me."

"She thinks I'm going to love you and leave you," he said shortly.

"Did you tell her that I was on board with that?"

"No. It's none of her business."

He scowled at the road, his mother's voice still echoing in his head. He wasn't going to apologize for having a broader horizon than her. And he definitely wasn't going to apologize or justify his private life. He always made sure that he was as honest as he could be with anyone he was involved with, and he'd had his fair share of wounded feelings and broken hearts over the years, too.

"It's very sweet of her to be so protective of me. Maybe I should have a word with her," Tara said. "Explain to her that we both know this is only temporary."

"It's none of her business," he said.

Her hand landed on his knee, warm and welcome. "It's still nice that she cares."

His shoulders dropped a notch as he let go of some of his irritation. "That's because you're a better person than I am."

"I've just had more experience dealing with a high-maintenance mom. Yours is a piece of cake compared to mine."

"True."

She squeezed his thigh. "Count your blessings."

She'd managed to tease a smile out of him by the time they turned into her street. Then Tara's own smile faded as she caught sight of the bright blue bomb parked in front of her townhouse.

Scarlett.

"Shit."

"What's wrong?" he asked.

"I forgot that Scarlett was coming over today to be here when Simon turns up to collect his stuff."

"You think she's been waiting long?"

"It's not that." Tara tugged on her ponytail nervously.

"What is it, then?"

"She'll see you."

Right. And that was a bad thing, apparently.

"Not that that's a bad thing," Tara said quickly, clearly picking up on his reaction. "It's just I was kind of hoping we could keep this just between you and me."

"And my parents."

"And your parents."

Scarlett had already exited her car and was standing watching them, arms crossed over her chest, her expression unreadable.

"Can I see you tonight?" he asked.

Truth be told, he didn't give a fat rat's caboose who knew about him and Tara, and that included the crew down at the station. She was the only thing that was important, nothing else.

"Um. Okay, if you want to."

"I want to." He leaned across the hand brake, palming the nape of her neck as he lowered his mouth to hers.

She tasted sweet, and she opened to him, her own hand coming up to tangle in his hair.

"What time should I come?" he asked when they finally parted.

"What time would you like to come over?"

"Early."

She smiled, the slightly-dazed look fading from her eyes. "Okay. I'll see you early, then."

She pressed a last kiss to his lips before grabbing her backpack and sliding from the truck.

He watched her walk over to greet her sister, aware of a deep reluctance within himself to let her go. It wasn't just because she'd be facing her ex today.

It felt as though he'd been waiting a life time for Tara

already.

Unsettled by his own thoughts, he headed for home.

"Wow. You are powering your way through the Fuck-it list, aren't you?" Scarlett said as Tara approached.

Tara couldn't quite interpret the expression on her sister's face. "Excuse me?"

"Have a fling with a hot guy. Remember that one?"

"Right." Tara had honestly forgotten that stupid list. After her day at the lake and her night with Reid, it didn't seem very important.

A day beneath the big Montana sky had put things back into perspective for her. The truth was, she liked most of her life, was comfortable with most of the choices she'd made.

And those she wasn't so happy with would be in the past once Simon had collected his things today.

Scarlett followed her as she let herself into the townhouse and dumped her backpack on the kitchen table.

"You know, I always wondered about you and Reid," Scarlett said.

"Did you?" It was news to Tara.

"Yeah, of course. He's hot, you guys are stuck in a car together all day. If it was me, I would have jumped him a long time ago."

"I was engaged, remember?"

Scarlett dismissed Simon with a flick of her fingers. Tara

couldn't help thinking that it would be nice to be able to do the same. She really wasn't looking forward to seeing him today. If she and Scarlett were identical twins, this would totally be a situation where she would be prepared for her sister to pretend to be her.

"So, has this been one of those simmering-beneath-the-surface things for the whole year you've worked together? Or did he just pounce on you out of nowhere? Or did you pounce on him…?"

Scarlett's eyes were bright with interest and Tara knew her well enough to understand where she was going with this.

"Don't get too excited. Reid is leaving Marietta soon, so this isn't a star-crossed lovers scenario."

She pulled her wet swimsuit and towel out of the backpack and went through to the laundry room to dump them in the washing machine.

When she turned around, Scarlett was standing in the doorway, and some of the sparkle had gone out of her eyes.

"Why is he leaving?"

"There's a job in Chicago. Also, he's a gypsy." She shrugged, offering her sister a wry smile.

"But you jumped into bed with him anyway?"

"I'm living on the wild side, remember?"

Her sister pursed her lips.

"What's wrong?" Tara asked.

"Are you sure you know what you're doing?"

"Of course. I'm going in with my eyes wide open. I'm going to have a good time with a great guy, and it's going to be okay when he heads off into the wild blue yonder."

Scarlett looked unconvinced.

"You don't believe me?" Tara asked.

"It's all great in theory, sweetie. But you didn't see your face when you got out of his truck just now."

"What about my face?"

"You looked happy. As though the lights were on, and someone was definitely home, and there was a party going on."

"I like him. So sue me. But I also know him, and I'm not stupid."

"Okay."

For some reason it was suddenly very important that she convince Scarlett that she meant every word that she said.

"He's got a second interview for a job on Tuesday, and when they offer him the job, they'll probably want him to start as soon as possible. So we're talking a couple of weeks, a month, before he's on his way. I can handle that."

Scarlett held up her hands. "Hey, I believe you. You've convinced me."

Tara narrowed her eyes, but she knew that if she kept pushing, she'd be getting into "doth protest too much" territory.

"You want me to start stacking the boxes near the door?" Scarlett said.

"No. He can lug them around. He's lucky that I packed his stuff up in the first place."

The house had been dotted with boxes and garbage bags full of stuff all week, and it would be good to have it gone.

"I heard that he's lost his job, as predicted."

"Good."

"I also heard something else, but I'm not sure if I should tell you or not." Scarlett tucked her fingers into the front pockets of her jeans as she waited for Tara's response.

"Tell me." Whatever it was, Tara could handle it.

"There's a rumor going around that Simon and Paige are engaged."

Tara set a hand on the cool metal of the washing machine. Simon was marrying her. That was…unexpected.

"Is she pregnant?"

"Who knows?" Scarlett moved closer, reaching out to rub her arm. "Sorry. But I thought you might hear it someplace else, or he might say something today, and I wanted you to be prepared."

"No, it's okay. I'm okay. It doesn't make any difference to me."

It really didn't. She'd made her peace with the mistake she'd almost made. Simon's betrayal wasn't any more or less palatable because he might end up married to a girl who was ten years his junior.

"Good," Scarlett said.

She told her sister about her day paddle boarding then,

and Scarlett told her that Mitch was due to land the day after tomorrow, having escorted his mother home and sorted out his affairs in Australia so he could join Scarlett in Montana permanently.

"Any leads on a place for the two of you yet?" Tara asked.

Scarlett had been living with their mother since she returned from Australia, not an ideal situation when you were a newly-wed woman.

"I found a place yesterday, actually. Where's your laptop?"

They were scrolling through the photographs on the local real estate website when a knock sounded. They both looked at the door, then each other.

"It must be douchebag o'clock," Scarlett said.

Tara smiled, reaching out to squeeze her sister's hand. It was good to have her here for this. Not something she would have necessarily said about her sister not so long ago. But Scarlett had changed—and maybe Tara had, too.

Taking a deep breath, she went to answer the door. Simon was standing on the other side, hands shoved into the pockets of his chinos, shoulders tense.

"We'll wait out on the deck while you clear your stuff," Tara said, not bothering with greetings.

She might be relieved that she wasn't going to marry this man, but that didn't excuse his bad behavior.

"I was hoping we could talk."

Tara crossed her arms over her chest. "About?"

"I wanted to explain. About Paige."

"I'm really not that interested, to be honest."

"I love her. We're going to move to Vegas, get married. Start over away from all of this."

Tara sent a silent thanks to her sister for forewarning her.

"I'm sure it will be a lovely ceremony. Don't forget the stuff in the garage."

She turned way and Simon stepped forward, reaching out to try to stop her. She shot him a look and his hand fell to his side. Nice to know he'd learned from last time.

"I'm sorry, Tara. I never meant for any of this to happen. For the record, I loved you. I loved you a lot. But the moment Paige walked into my class room at the start of the year I knew I was in trouble. I can't explain it better than that, I'm sorry."

He looked so tortured, guilty and stressed that for a second she felt a little sorry for him. But only a second.

"You're not the man I thought you were," she said. "You lied. You abused the trust of a student. You betrayed me. I don't know what you want me to say to you, but I'm not going to give you a free pass, Simon."

"I don't want that. I know what I did was shitty and wrong."

"Good. Then we're on the same page. Like I said, we'll be on the deck if you need anything."

Scarlett gave Simon a scathing head to toe before turning

and leading the way to the deck. Tara actually had a smile on her face by the time they were outside in the early morning sunshine.

"You have to teach me how to do that sometime. I swear, I could hear his balls shriveling," Tara said.

Scarlett looked at little startled by her laughter. Then she smiled, too.

"That's my Medusa look. I use it on grabby employers. It's all in the lip. You have to get a little curl in it, and look down your nose."

By the time Simon had cleared the house of his things and rapped on the back door to let them know he was done, Tara had mastered the Medusa look. She was tempted to try it out on Simon, but her heart wasn't in it.

She was better off without him, in so many ways.

"Well. I guess this is it," Simon said on the front porch.

"Yep. I'll send you your share of the security deposit sometime next week," Tara said.

"Keep it. It's the least I owe you."

"I'll send it," she said firmly.

He nodded, then glanced at the ground. His throat bobbed a couple of times, and when he looked back up at her his eyes were glassy with tears. "I'm sorry. I'm going to miss you."

She stared at him for a long moment. He really was an idiot. A messed up, foolish idiot who had made a lot of really dumb moves.

"I hope it works out for you," she said. Otherwise all of this, all the ugliness and hurt and embarrassment would be for nothing.

He nodded, then turned and headed down the stairs.

Tara shut the door and leaned against it, waiting for him to go. She was aware of her sister watching her. Together they waited until the sound of Simon's car had faded.

"Well, that's that, I guess," Tara said, pushing away from the door.

Scarlett came and put her arms around her. "You're my hero. If ever this happens to me, if I can be one tenth as classy as you, I will be so proud of myself."

Tara blinked away sudden tears. Not because she was sad about Simon, but because she knew she was lucky. She had good people around her. People who loved and cared about her.

They held each other tightly for a long beat, then eased apart.

"Now, how do you feel about driving me over to The Wolves Den so I can collect my pickup?" Tara asked.

REID SPENT THE day working with his father in the orchard. His thoughts were on Tara almost the whole time, mulling over the things she'd said to him and the time they'd spent together last night.

At four he went up to the apartment and pulled out his

suit, checking to make sure he didn't need to get it dry-cleaned before his interview on Tuesday. It was fine, and he hung it with a fresh shirt, ready to be ironed the night before his departure—he'd already booked flights, and he planned to leave early Tuesday and get back late the same night.

He was aware of a heaviness within himself as he contemplated the whole process. The flight, the interview, all the jumping through flaming hoops that would be required of him. Then he reminded himself that it was a great job, and an excellent opportunity. Three times the money he could make at Bozeman PD, and he'd be living in the vibrant, cosmopolitan city of Chicago.

He walked to the window and stood staring out at the orchard. Trees stretched into the distance in orderly lines, branches swaying in the wind. He knew from his time out there today that the fruit was coming along nicely. Soon it would be harvest time and they'd be opening the orchard to the public.

His mother hadn't raised the prospect of selling to the Dearborns again, and he had no idea if she'd spoken to his father about it.

It's not just going to go away because you want it to.

He turned away from the view and headed for the bathroom, stripping his sweaty work clothes and stepping beneath the shower. He took the time to shave carefully, splashing on aftershave before pulling on his good jeans and a linen shirt he'd bought in Rome.

He admitted to himself that he was nervous as he drove to Tara's place. He wasn't sure why. He wanted to see her very badly. Wanted to hold her again. Touch her. Look into her eyes. He was also aware of the clock ticking. All modesty aside, he knew he had a good shot at the Chicago job. Which meant his time with Tara would be limited.

The moment he acknowledged the thought, he started coming up with out clauses for himself. There was no reason, for example, why he couldn't fly home a couple of times a month to see her and help his folks out. She might be willing to fly out to Chicago, too. She'd talked about wanting to travel more as they floated around Fairy Lake. Maybe they could manage a long distance thing for a while.

And then what? a voice asked in the back of his head.

Long distance was only worth enduring if there was the prospect of an end in sight. And it was pretty well established that Tara was not about to uproot herself from Marietta.

She opened the door when she heard his car in the driveway, watching as he exited the truck. Her hair was up, and she'd put on a little makeup, making her eyes smoky and sexy and her mouth pink.

She looked good enough to eat.

"Hi," she said. "How was your—"

He stole the rest of her words with a kiss, his arms wrapping around her, hands gravitating to her perky little ass. She gave a murmur of approval as he backed her toward the doorway.

He had her top off by the time they'd reached the couch, and seconds later her bra was off, too. Filling his hands with creamy smooth flesh, he tongued her nipples and relished the way she trembled in response. She started fumbling at his belt buckle, pushing her hands into his jeans. He broke from her briefly to push them all the way down, helping her do the same, then he set her on the arm of the couch and slid inside her. She wrapped her legs around him, kissing him avidly as he began to move.

"You feel so good," he whispered in her ear. "I want to do this forever."

"Yes."

He reached between them to find the place she needed him the most, stroking her inside and out until she tightened around him, her knees gripping his hips. Only then did he let himself go, pleasure swamping him.

She pressed a kiss to his chest afterward, and he wondered if she could hear his still-pounding heart.

"I guess it's lucky my sister went home earlier, huh?" she said.

She tilted her head to look up at him, her face full of laughter, and his chest got tight the way it had that morning when he'd looked into her eyes.

If he got the job, he was going to be walking away from this woman.

Good luck with that one.

Chapter Ten

THE NEXT THREE weeks were the most bittersweet of Tara's life. She spent the remaining week of her leave helping out with her mother, reorganizing the townhouse and spending time with Reid. He took her paddle-boarding again, this time to Ennis Lake, and they made love on the shore beneath the warm sun. By mutual consent they didn't talk about his job interview much, apart from general details. Reid didn't seem eager to hash it over, and she wasn't sure she could maintain the pretense that she would be happy for him if he got it.

The night before she was due back on the job, they had a discussion about the potential weirdness of their work situation. They both agreed that there was nothing they could do but wing it and trust each other, as they always had.

Tara turned up the following morning feeling crazy nervous and very exposed, albeit in a very different way from the day after she'd found out about Simon. Her colleagues were pleased to see her, however, and there was nothing in Reid's greeting or demeanor to let on that she was anything more to him than his patrol partner.

She did her best to hold up her end of the deal, even though it was hard when she was so vitally aware of everything about him. The sheen of his hair, the warmth in his eyes, the texture of his skin. His smell, the way he walked, the timbre of his voice.

After twenty minutes in the patrol car, however, ingrained habit and instinct kicked in. They were on the job, and anything else between them fell back a step as they went about their duties. It helped that she'd always respected him—looked up to him, really—as a cop, and that they were kept busy with the usual rash of complaints. Break-ins, domestic disputes, MVAs. It was different, working together now they were lovers, but it wasn't difficult or impossible. Best of all, she was confident that none of their colleagues or superiors had a clue what was going on between them, which was just the way she liked it. She'd had enough of being the source of department scuttlebutt. She was more than happy to cede the floor to someone else's life dramas.

She helped out on the orchard whenever there was work to be done, enjoying spending time with Reid without having to monitor her behavior. His parents were so welcoming, she caught herself on the verge of explaining the finite nature of her relationship with Reid half a dozen times, but each time she reminded herself that they knew about the Chicago job. They knew Reid would be leaving soon.

Reid surprised her by offering to help out at her mom's

place, too, taking it upon himself to mow her lawns and do a few odd jobs around the place that neither she nor Scarlett had felt up to. Mitch was good to pitch in, too, and the Buck women found themselves in the novel position of having two healthy, strong men at their bidding. Watching Reid and Mitch joke around with each other and her mom was but one of many moments that made Tara acutely aware of the hole Reid was going to leave in her life when he finally packed up and went.

But she'd known that, going in. She was prepared for it.

At least, she thought she was.

Then she woke on a Sunday morning almost three weeks exactly after Reid had taken her to Fairy Lake, and slipped from the bed to make use of the facilities. On her way back, she diverted to the kitchen to turn the coffee maker on. She was about to pad back to bed, her head full of all the delicious ways she could wake her lover, when her gaze fell on the thick envelope sitting on the kitchen counter. The Klieg Security Group logo filled the top left corner, and she found herself taking a step closer.

Don't, a voice in her head said, but she was already lifting it. It was empty, its contents sitting beneath it on the counter. She stared at the bold words across the top of the page. Confidential Employment Contract.

So.

Her gaze went to the postage mark on the envelope. It was dated earlier in the week, which meant Reid had been sitting on this news for at least a couple of days.

You knew this was coming.

She did. She'd prepared herself for it a dozen times. But nothing she'd imagined came even close to the way she felt right now—as though the bottom had fallen out of her world.

Which was stupid. So stupid.

She pressed a hand to her stomach, blinking rapidly to dispel the tears that were burning at the back of her eyes.

She was going to lose him.

The pain of the realization was visceral, like a blow to the solar plexus.

Which, again, was so dumb. This wasn't an ambush. She'd bought into their fling knowing it would end, and soon. Now it was time to pay the piper.

She set the envelope back on top of the contract and turned to the sink, running herself a glass of water. Her hand shook as she lifted it to her mouth.

I didn't think he'd go.

She closed her eyes as she admitted the truth to herself. Even though she knew Reid, even though he'd regaled her with tales of his travels, his eyes bright as he described a bazaar in Turkey or a weekend market in Paris, she'd sold herself a secret fantasy where Reid decided that he'd had enough of seeing the world, that being with her was more important than any of that. And she'd bought it, hook, line, and sinker, because she was wildly, crazily, passionately in love with him and didn't want to let him go.

You fool.

She set the half-full glass on the drainer, unable to swallow past the lump of emotion in her throat.

For a moment she was so overwhelmed by the loss she was about to endure that the urge to sink to the floor and curl into a ball was almost irresistible.

Her mother had been like that after her father left, she remembered. She'd sobbed until her eyes were so red and puffy they were almost raw, she'd refused food, she'd spent hours in bed, not talking to anyone. Standing in Reid's kitchen, for the first time in her life Tara truly understood her mother's helplessness in the face of her grief.

It would be very easy to let the pain take over, as her mother had, to succumb to it and let it swamp her. Right now, it felt like a tsunami crashing down on her, unavoidable, sweeping everything in its path.

But Tara was not her mother. She'd worked diligently all her life to be different. She'd trained herself to be disciplined, to be capable. To be resilient. She was resilient.

She would be okay when Reid left. It would hurt. It would hurt like hell. But she would be okay. There would be no sleeping for days on end for her. She wouldn't abandon herself to pain. She couldn't.

Her knuckles were aching, and when she looked down she realized she was gripping the edge of the sink so tightly her fingers were white. She forced herself to let go. Suddenly the need to be outside, away from Reid, was so strong that she didn't dare disobey it.

She'd brought her running gear with her last night in anticipation of a cross-country outing with Reid today. She would put it on and slip out and run until this feeling in her chest—this tight, suffocating, painful heaviness—was gone. And when she came back, she would wait until he told her his good news and she would be happy for him.

She would.

She walked quietly into the bedroom to collect the bag with her running gear. Reid was sprawled across the mattress, the sheet tangled around his hips. She stood looking at him for a long moment, aware of the urge to climb into bed beside him and cling to him. Maybe if she asked, he would stay. Maybe if she begged him.

She retreated to the kitchen before she could allow the thought to take root. She pulled on underwear, fastening her sports bra with cold, fumbling hands. Then she pulled on her running leggings and a tank top, and finally her shoes and socks. She tied her hair back into a ponytail, then took a moment to leave a quick note on the pad of paper near the phone.

Felt the urge to run. See you soon, sleepyhead. T.

She left the note propped against the coffee can and made her way to the door.

"Where are you going?"

She glanced over her shoulder to find Reid standing

there in all his naked glory, one arm raised to scratch his head. It said a lot that even now, when she was on the verge of falling apart, she still felt the burn of attraction as she looked at his beautiful body.

She forced a smile. "I'm just ducking out for a quick run," she said. "Just felt the urge."

"Give me five and I'll come with you."

"That's okay. You go back to bed. We can still go out together later."

She loved their runs together, and she wasn't about to give one up when it might very well be their last.

"Don't be silly. I'll be two minutes, tops." He closed the distance between them, wrapping her in his arms and his smell and his warmth.

She kissed him, swallowing the burn of tears. She couldn't object without crying. Without losing it. And she didn't want to lose it.

Not with him, anyway.

"Okay."

She hovered by the door as he pulled on running shorts and a tank top, sitting on the couch to tug on socks and his shoes. He ducked into the bathroom to stick his head under the tap and gulp down a glass of water, then he was back with her, his eyes alert now as he studied her.

"Is everything all right?" he asked, and she knew that he could sense her tension and upset.

He'd always been tuned into her. Always.

"Yep. Just feel like blowing the cobwebs away."

She led the way down the steps, going through the motions of doing some warmup stretches even though she really just wanted to run.

And then they were heading up the driveway, the gravel hard underfoot, and the terrible pressing-down feeling seemed to recede as she picked up the pace.

Very deliberately she cleared her mind, concentrating on her stride and her breathing, feeling the stretch in her hips with each step, visualizing her mid-foot hitting the ground and pushing off again.

Her muscles became liquid and warm as she slipped into the groove. The wind rushing past her felt good, the burn in her legs and lungs felt good, the perfect distraction from the hollowness inside her. She increased the pace, barely looking at Reid as she pushed harder and harder.

Then, somehow, she was sprinting, arms and legs pumping, her whole body on fire as she ran as fast, as hard as she could. Her feet slapped the ground, her eyes streamed, every muscle and sinew screamed for relief.

Still she kept running, relishing the burn, embracing the pain because it was so much easier than dealing with the hurt inside herself.

I love him, I love him, I love him. Don't leave me, don't leave me, don't leave me.

And suddenly she couldn't breathe, and she couldn't see, and she had to stop as tears flooded her eyes and her throat.

She staggered to a halt, gasping for air, her chest heaving with sobs, tears pouring down her face.

"Tara." Reid was panting, too, his face twisted with concern as he reached for her.

She shook her head, unable to accept his comfort when she wanted—needed—it so badly. His hands fell to his sides as he frowned, his gaze never leaving her face.

"What's going on?"

She turned her back on him, walking a few paces away, trying to get a grip. But the words she wanted to say were rising up inside her, and she couldn't stop them, even though pride and history and experience told her they were pointless.

"Would it make a difference if I asked you to stay?" she said, her back still to him.

"Tara."

His arms came around her from behind, his big body enveloping hers. His arms were like steel bands, and she felt the rasp of his morning beard against her cheek as he pressed his face alongside hers.

"You don't need to ask. I'm not going anywhere, doofus."

She frowned, not understanding. "I saw the contract, Reid."

She struggled free from his grip, turning to face him. Needing to see him.

"I called them on Thursday and told them I didn't want

it."

Reid's dark eyes were steady on her as he waited for her response.

"But you don't want to live in Marietta. You can't imagine your life playing out here."

"That was before us. Before I understood that what I've been looking for all my life is right here. Tara, I love you. I've been crazy about you since the moment I met you. Wherever you are is where I want to be. It's that simple."

She shook her head. It wasn't that simple. Her father had been like Reid, a born gypsy. Restless. Always wanting more. He'd handled being domesticated for thirteen years before his nature had gotten the better of him.

"I'm not going to make the same mistake my mother made," she said. "You want to be out there. You love exploring new places. What is there for you in Marietta, besides me?"

"My parents. The orchard. Mountains. Lakes. A life with you by my side. The children we will have together. Believe me, that trumps Rome or Egypt or Mumbai every time, Tara."

She shook her head again. She wanted to believe him. He was offering her everything, her heart's desire. But she couldn't believe him. She couldn't.

He reached out and caught her hand, pulling her close, his other hand reaching up to tilt her chin so he could look into her eyes.

"Let me tell you the way I see this working. My parents move into town, and we take over the house. Anything you want to change, you change, with my blessing. I've got some savings, and we sink a bit of money into modernizing some of the machinery to make things easier. We both take our detective's exam, and when the time comes when we want to have kids, we work it out between us. Maybe I take some time out, then you take some time out. Whatever. And at least once a year, we turn our backs on all of this, and we go somewhere just for us. Somewhere new, somewhere we can discover together."

"Stop it," she said, desperately trying to hang onto her hard-earned sense of self-preservation.

"You don't like any of that? Fine. The only part that's not negotiable for me is you. I've gotten a lot of things ass-backwards in my life, Tara, but this is right. I love you, and I will always love you. You are my future. Only you."

He was holding her face in both his hands now, his thumbs brushing her tears away.

"I want to believe you so much," she whispered.

"Then believe, baby. I promise that if you fall, I will catch you. And I know you'll do the same for me."

Tara felt dizzy, as though some fundamental anchor within herself had just snapped free. If she did this and it didn't work out—if they tried and failed—the pain she'd just stared in the eye would be nothing.

If Reid left her, it would destroy her. She would become

her mother.

Reid leaned forward and kissed her lips, and she tasted the salt of his sweat and her tears, and she felt the gentleness in his hands, and when he pulled back she saw the fierce love in his eyes.

"I love you," she said.

"I know, sweetheart. I love you like crazy. I love you so much I'm going to pretend I don't mind about that damned motorbike, and I cannot wait to start my life with you."

He kissed her again, deeply this time, his tongue stroking hers, one hand palming the nape of her neck, the other sliding down her back to urge her closer. She felt his arousal against her belly, and the flare of her own desire, and knew that even though she was terrified, even though life had taught her that this was the most dangerous thing she would ever do, she couldn't not do it.

To do so would make a lie of everything she had ever tried to be, and mean she would be turning her back on a man who filled her with love and pride and heat and need.

"Yes," she said. "Yes. Let's do it. All of it. The house, the exams, the babies, all of it. All of it."

"Good answer," he said, and then he kissed her to seal their deal.

Epilogue

One Year Later

"I'M GOING TO bed now, but you are not to touch anything, Tara, do you hear me?" Tammy Buck said as she pushed herself upright from her seat. Bottles of nail polish, emery boards and polish scattered the kitchen table in front of her, along with a number of soiled cotton balls. "The last thing we want to be doing is fixing your nails tomorrow when you'll have a million better things to do."

"Like getting married," Scarlett chimed in.

Tara waggled her fingers in the air. "I'll be good, I promise."

"You did a good job, Scarlett. There's a career there if you want it," her mother said approvingly. Between them, she and Scarlett had transformed Tara's nails from workaday practical to wedding glamorous, shaping them and buffing them and finally painting them with a pale pink varnish that was pearlescent in the overhead light.

"I would be high as a kite on all those fumes, Mom. And all I did was follow your expert instructions," Scarlett said.

"Don't blow smoke up my skirt, I know how good I am. At least, how good I used to be."

Tara resisted the urge to offer to escort her mother to bed. In recent months, her mother had reached a sort of peace with her illness, and a new independence had grown out of her acceptance. These days, she liked to do as much for herself as she could, claiming that there would be plenty of opportunities for them to fuss over her in the future.

Scarlett waited until they heard the bedroom door click shut before standing.

"You want some of the good stuff now?"

"Yes, please."

Their mother preferred sweet spumante, always had, but Scarlett had bought a bottle of French champagne to celebrate Tara's last night as a single woman.

The pop of the champagne cork echoed in the kitchen, and Tara accepted a brimming, frothing glass from her sister.

"To sunny skies tomorrow and for the rest of your lives," Scarlett said, raising her glass in toast.

They clinked glasses, both making appreciative noises as they swallowed a mouthful of yeasty, dry goodness.

"So good," Tara said.

"You nervous?" Scarlett asked.

Tara shook her head instantly. "No. Excited, but not nervous."

Tomorrow, she was going to become Mrs. Reid Dalton, and the next stage of their life together would begin. While the thought of all the theater of tomorrow's wedding made her feel a little twitchy, she didn't have a single doubt about the man she would be marrying.

He was her rock, her heart, her everything. She adored him. She admired him. She lusted after him. She couldn't wait to walk down the aisle and make her vows.

"You love him," Scarlett said in a childish, sing-song teasing voice.

"Yep," Tara said, grinning unashamedly.

"Good thing Mr. Douchebag had a thing for cheerleaders, then, huh?"

Tara shuddered as she thought about the terrible mistake she'd almost made.

"Don't remind me. I was such an idiot."

"You had your reasons," Scarlett said, her green eyes warm with understanding and acceptance.

Tara felt a rush of love for her twin. For so many years, they had pulled against one another, each attempting to carve her own place in the world. Somehow, though, their mother's illness and the changes in their personal lives had led to a new accord between them. Scarlett had let go of the need to always be the rebel and the entertainer, and Tara had resigned from her role as family protector. For the first time since they were little, they were friends, and it felt good.

"You want some chocolate, too?" Scarlett asked.

She was already on her feet, heading for the pantry. Tara smiled at her sister's fluffy-bunny slippers, paired with a pair of rather sexy shorty pajamas.

"You wear that outfit at home?" she couldn't help asking.

"Hell no. Mitch won't let me wear anything to bed. He's an impatient man."

Tara laughed.

Scarlett returned with a big box of chocolates bearing the Copper Mountain Chocolates logo, sliding the lid off as she placed it in front of Tara.

"Wow," Tara said, surveying the decadent array in front of her. Sage Carrigan's chocolates were legendary in Marietta, and there were enough here to make her teeth ache.

Scarlett passed her the little booklet which told her which chocolate was which. "Save me a coffee cream, but the Turkish Delights are all yours."

"I thought you loved Turkish Delights," Tara said, looking up from studying the booklet. She could remember having to strategize like crazy to get her share as a kid.

"Nope. Dad was the one who loved them, remember?"

She said it so matter-of-factly, but the mention of their father stole the smile from Tara's lips. Even though it had been a long time since he'd been a part of her life, she'd been haunted by thoughts of him lately. Only natural, perhaps, in the lead-up to the wedding, but a little disconcerting, too.

She picked a caramel from the box and passed the guide to her sister.

"Did you miss him at your wedding?" she asked quietly.

Scarlett took a second to answer. "I thought about him. I

didn't miss him. He's been gone so long, I can't really remember what it was like to have him in my life."

"Yeah." Tara pushed the tray of chocolates away.

"Hey. You okay?" Scarlett's forehead was wrinkled with concern.

"I need to tell you something. But I'm scared you'll hate me," Tara confessed.

"I will never hate you. Ever.".

Tara glanced down into her lap at her perfect pearly nails.

"A month before Dad left, I came home from school and caught him and Wendy in the kitchen."

Scarlett blinked a couple of times, processing. Then she mouthed a four letter word. "What did he say?"

"He cried. Told me it was a one-off." Tara reached for her champagne glass and took a big gulp to ease her dry throat. "He told me it would never happen again, and made me promise not to tell Mom."

"What an asshole."

It was so not what Tara had been expecting she almost laughed. It came out as a sort of hiccup, and she had to blink away tears again. Scarlett was watching her closely, her head tilted to one side.

"Wait a minute. You were worried I'd hate you because of this?" Scarlett asked, her tone incredulous.

"When we came home that day and he was gone and Mom was crying with Aunt Margot… It took me ages to accept that Dad wasn't coming back. That he'd lied to me. And Mom kept on saying that she'd had no warning, no idea that it had all come out of the blue, and all I could think was that if I'd told her what I'd seen, maybe they could have fixed things…" She broke off to wipe away the single tear that had found its way down her cheek.

"God. And you've been carrying that around all these years. If I knew where he was, I'd hunt him down and kick him somewhere it hurts," Scarlett said fiercely. "Tara, you were a kid, and he was a liar and a cheat and too charming for his own good. Everything that happened was his fault. All of it."

"I know that. I do. I just…There will always be that question inside me, you know?" Tara said.

Scarlett scooted her chair closer and wrapped her arms around Tara.

"Let it go, Tara Banana. Let it go."

Scarlett hadn't used the childish nickname for years, and Tara had to blink away more tears as her sister embraced her.

"You have been an amazing sister, the backbone of this family," Scarlett said. "When I think of all the shit Mom and I have put you through over the years… please don't blame yourself for his selfishness. Please don't think that that was anything to do with you."

Her sister's words were a balm, the forgiveness and acceptance that Tara had needed for fourteen years. Resting her chin on her sister's shoulder, Tara let herself cry, clinging to her twin.

"I love you so much," she said brokenly.

"Back at you, baby. So back at you," Scarlett said.

They were both red-eyed and wet-cheeked when they drew apart. Scarlett sniffed and used the back of her hand to wipe her face.

"Boy do we know how to party," she said dryly.

Tara smiled, and the next thing she knew she was laughing. Scarlett watched her with a bemused smile.

"You okay there?"

"Yes. I think so. How about you?"

"I'm good."

They smiled at each other, then Scarlett nudged the box of chocolates toward her. "You get another pick now because you're so tragic," she said.

Tara shot her a mock-outraged look. "I'm going to take it, too."

She made a big deal out of searching for the coffee creams, making lots of yum noises when she bit into one. Scarlett commandeered the box then, stockpiling the remaining coffee creams in a pile in front of her.

"Can I ask you something?" Tara asked as she watched her sister be a pig. "Do you think I should tell Mom?"

Scarlett was silent for a moment as she considered the question. Then she shook her head. "I don't see the point. It will only upset her, and it won't change anything."

The last of the weight Tara had been carrying lifted from

her shoulders.

"Reid told me I should talk to you about it," she admitted.

"He's a smart guy. Great taste in women, looks hot in jeans. You should totally marry him as soon as you can."

Tara smiled. "That's a good idea. Why didn't I think of it?"

"Because I'm the ideas twin."

"Right, that must be it."

They talked till midnight, then Tara went to bed in her old bedroom and stared at the ceiling, chocolate, champagne and emotion buzzing through her body. Finally she drifted off to sleep, waking early the next morning. The nerves she'd denied last night made a late appearance, and she went for a quick run to burn off some adrenaline before jumping into the shower. She and Scarlett did each other's makeup, then their mothers, then Mitch arrived looking outrageously good in a dark suit.

"Good God am I glad you married me," Scarlett said, kissing him hello.

Mitch gave her an appreciative head to toe. "Am I allowed to touch any of this or is it for display only?"

He didn't wait for an answer, dropping a kiss onto her lips.

Tara cleared her throat. "If you don't mind, I'd like to hit the road. I believe there's a certain someone counting on me turning up."

Mitch let out a whistle when he saw her. "Looking good, Mrs. Dalton. Someone's going to be very happy to see you."

Tara blushed, pleased. She was excited for Reid to see her in her figure hugging, lacy gown, complete with a modest train. She felt beautiful, and she hoped he would think she was, too.

Mitch ushered them out to the car, helping their Mom into the front seat while Scarlett helped Tara wrangle her gown into the back. Tara's belly danced with butterflies during the short drive to the orchard. The front gate was decorated with white balloons that danced on their strings as they drove past. Tara could see the snowy white peaks of the tent that had been erected for their reception as they stopped in front of the house. Scarlett helped her out, and Tara took a moment to catch her breath and arrange her veil before her sister passed her her flowers.

"Okay, let's do this," Tara said.

Walking slowly in deference to their mother's compromised gait and Tara's long gown, they rounded the house and emerged on the lawn where chairs had been set up in front of a garden archway covered with flowering apricot roses. The celebrant stood beneath it, a tall, dark-haired, broad shouldered man by his side, his back to the gathered guests.

The violinist they'd hired for the ceremony started playing when he caught Tara's eye, and the dark-haired man turned.

Tara looked down the aisle at the man she was about to marry and couldn't stop her mouth from curling into a smile. An answering smile curved Reid's mouth, and warmth expanded in her chest. This man made her so happy. So happy. Thank God she'd been brave enough to trust his love.

Her heart keeping time with the music, a warm breeze tugging at her veil, she took her first step toward her future.

THE END

If you enjoyed **Almost a Bride**, you'll love the other Great Wedding Giveaway stories!

What a Bride Wants by Kelly Hunter

Second Chance Bride by Trish Morey

The Unexpected Bride by Joanne Walsh

The Cowboy's Reluctant Bride by Katherine Garbera

A Game of Brides by Megan Crane

The Substitute Bride by Kathleen O'Brien

Last Year's Bride by Anne McAllister

The Make-Believe Wedding by Sarah Mayberry

Available now at your favorite online retailer!

ABOUT THE AUTHOR

Sarah Mayberry is the award winning, best selling author of more than 30 books. She lives by the bay in Melbourne with her husband and a small, furry Cavoodle called Max. When she isn't writing romance, Sarah writes scripts for television as well as working on other film and TV projects. She loves to cook, knows she should tend to her garden more, and considers curling up with a good book the height of luxury.

Visit her website at www.sarahmayberry.com.

Thank you for reading

ALMOST A BRIDE

If you enjoyed this book, you can find more from all our great authors at TulePublishing.com, or from your favorite online retailer.

Printed in Great Britain
by Amazon